CITY OF SECRETS

More Warhammer from Black Library

HALLOWED KNIGHTS: PLAGUE GARDEN
Josh Reynolds

EIGHT LAMENTATIONS: SPEAR OF SHADOWS
Josh Reynolds

OVERLORDS OF THE IRON DRAGON
C L Werner

HAMMERHAL
Josh Reynolds

WARHAMMER®
CHRONICLES

• THE LEGEND OF SIGMAR •
Graham McNeill
BOOK ONE: Heldenhammer
BOOK TWO: Empire
BOOK THREE: God King

• THE RISE OF NAGASH •
Mike Lee
BOOK ONE: Nagash the Sorcerer
BOOK TWO: Nagash the Unbroken
BOOK THREE: Nagash Immortal

• THE VAMPIRE WARS •
Steven Savile
BOOK ONE: Inheritance
BOOK TWO: Dominion
BOOK THREE: Retribution

• THE SUNDERING •
Gav Thorpe
BOOK ONE: Malekith
BOOK TWO: Shadow King
BOOK THREE: Caledor

• CHAMPIONS OF CHAOS •
*Darius Hinks, Sarah Cawkwell &
Ben Counter*
BOOK ONE: Sigvald
BOOK TWO: Valkia the Bloody
BOOK THREE: Van Horstmann

CITY OF SECRETS

NICK HORTH

BLACK LIBRARY

A BLACK LIBRARY PUBLICATION

First published in Great Britain in 2016 by
Black Library
This edition published in Great Britain in 2018 by
Black Library,
Games Workshop Ltd.,
Willow Road,
Nottingham,
NG7 2WS, UK.

10 9 8 7 6 5 4 3 2 1

Produced by Games Workshop in Nottingham.
Cover illustration by Mark Holmes.

A CIP record for this book is available from the British Library.

ISBN 13: 978-1-78496-751-2

See Black Library on the internet at

blacklibrary.com

Find out more about Games Workshop
and the worlds of Warhammer at

games-workshop.com

Printed and bound by CPI Group (UK) Ltd, Croydon, CR0 4YY

From the maelstrom of a sundered world, the
Eight Realms were born. The formless and the divine
exploded into life.

Strange, new worlds appeared in the firmament, each one
gilded with spirits, gods and men. Noblest of the gods was
Sigmar. For years beyond reckoning he illuminated the realms,
wreathed in light and majesty as he carved out his reign. His
strength was the power of thunder. His wisdom was infinite.
Mortal and immortal alike kneeled before his lofty throne.
Great empires rose and, for a while, treachery was banished.
Sigmar claimed the land and sky as his own and ruled over a
glorious age of myth.

But cruelty is tenacious. As had been foreseen, the great
alliance of gods and men tore itself apart. Myth and legend
crumbled into Chaos. Darkness flooded the realms. Torture,
slavery and fear replaced the glory that came before. Sigmar
turned his back on the mortal kingdoms, disgusted by their
fate. He fixed his gaze instead on the remains of the world he
had lost long ago, brooding over its charred core, searching
endlessly for a sign of hope. And then, in the dark heat of
his rage, he caught a glimpse of something magnificent. He
pictured a weapon born of the heavens. A beacon powerful
enough to pierce the endless night. An army hewn from
everything he had lost.

Sigmar set his artisans to work and for long ages they toiled,
striving to harness the power of the stars. As Sigmar's great
work neared completion, he turned back to the realms and saw
that the dominion of Chaos was almost complete. The hour
for vengeance had come. Finally, with lightning blazing across
his brow, he stepped forth to unleash his creations.

The Age of Sigmar had begun.

ACT ONE

The prophecy promised slaughter and death, and so the Stormcast Eternals marched to war.

The city of Excelsis watched them leave her borders. All along the great walls the lightning engines spun and whirred, sending flickering cascades of storm energy coruscating across the sky. It was a fitting salute. Beneath the churning aether, columns of solemn warriors marched under the panoply of their Warrior Chambers. Their splendid, gilded war-plate bore many colours. There was the pristine white with blue trim of the Knights Excelsior, most zealous of Sigmar's sons. Elsewhere could be seen the grim black of the Sons of Mallus, a Stormhost whose temperament was as sombre as their aspect. Ahead, always ahead, was the sea-green of the Knights of the Aurora.

It had been the first prophecy in a decade to bring the city's war council together. The Prophesiers had conversed with the mages of the Collegiate, and both had ratified the augury, mined from the deepest veins of the Spear of Mallus – the colossal shard of fate-touched rock that aeons ago had plunged into the Realm of Beasts and ripped from the earth the very bay upon which Excelsis now stood. This was truth, they said. There was no question.

The orruks were gathering, and in numbers large enough to engulf a city.

And so the Stormcasts marched. The fortified gates of the city rumbled open, and the columns of towering figures snaked off into the low hills and deadly plains of the Coast of Tusks.

'Do they eat, do you think?' said Custin.

The boy was greeted with a volley of blank stares. Rare was the minute when the stick-thin guardsman wasn't asking some damn fool question or another.

'The lightning men,' he continued, scratching his pointed chin, which was as ever covered with a fine blanket of wispy hair that was as close to a beard as he could manage. 'My cousin Rullig, he says they do. Says they order up a big cart full of salted meat to their fortress every other market day. Now my other cousin, Ullig, he says that's nonsense. Swears he's seen them in the early hours, up on the high wall eating thunder and lightning. The lightning strikes and they just swallow it up.'

'Sigmar's bones, boy,' sighed old Happer, leaning back on his bunk and staring at the stone above his head. Once grey, it was now stained a sickly yellow, a result of the pipe that constantly rested between his lips. 'You've a rare talent for talking nonsense.'

'Leave the lad be,' said Corporal Armand Callis, stifling a yawn as he sat up on his bunk. 'We can't all be as wise as you, Happer. Not for a good few decades yet, anyway.'

Happer snorted indignantly. 'Boy's been fed too many tall tales. I've lived long enough to know the Eternals ain't no fairy-tale knights. I ever tell you about the purges, son? I've seen things that would make your guts turn to ice.'

From the other side of the room came an exasperated groan, and a balled-up sock arced across to strike Happer on the side of the head.

'Spare me another tale of the bloody White Angels,' said Longholme, running a hand through her greasy black hair. 'I've heard a hundred times how they're going to come at night and steal us all away, damn us all as heretics and stick our heads on the harbour wall.'

Happer opened his mouth to reply, but instead just shook his head and muttered darkly under his breath.

Custin sighed and crossed to the window. 'Raining heavy now,' he said, looking out glumly. 'We're to get soaked.'

From outside the heavy wooden door to the barracks, hurried footsteps could be heard. Shortly after, Jammud came bursting into the room, breathless from taking the stairs two or three at a time.

'Corporal?' he said, panting at the exertion. 'The sarge is sick again. His belly, he says. He can't make patrol tonight.'

Callis hauled himself to his feet, biting back a curse. If Sergeant Ames spent less time stuffing his ever-expanding guts with dock cakes and cheap liquor, and more time earning his blasted rank, then maybe he wouldn't be bedridden four nights out of seven. Of course, Ames would be the one earning twenty more glimmerings a week while Callis did his job for him, so who was the real fool here? He buckled on his breastplate and tucked his pistol into the shoulder holster beneath his long overcoat. The black powder weapon would have to be kept dry. A lowly corporal could never afford one of those fancy duardin-made wheel-lock guns that kept out moisture – his sidearm was usually a trusty piece, but a sniff of rainwater and he might as well be wielding a loaf of bread.

He pushed the bitterness deep down inside, adding it to his not inconsiderable stock, and jammed his sabre into the scabbard at his side.

'All right, you lot,' he barked. 'On your feet. You know the drill here. We make our circuit, we do our best to avoid getting our pockets picked, and we get back here by the early morning for a couple of hours sleep before we have to do it all over again.'

There was the expected chorus of grumbles and moans. Callis strode across to Custin and peered out of the window of the Coldguard Bastion. The young guardsman was right; it was a torrential downpour. Thick spears of rain, the kind that almost hurt when they hit you. The Bastion loomed over the eastern harbour side of Excelsis, an uncompromising slab of stone littered with gun emplacements and watchtowers. The massive cannons on top of the structure had range and power enough to defend the entire bay. That was the Coldguard Regiment's unglamorous task, while the Stormblessed, the Bronze Claws and other elite units made their forays into the wilderness alongside the Stormcasts, earning glories and battle honours.

Callis sighed. Guard duty was all soldiers longed for while on manoeuvres outside the city walls, but give it a season or two and you had a fortress full of bored troops on your hands, all with glimmerings to spare. Patrolling and constant drills were all you had to occupy them. And, if you happened to be a young corporal with a drunken sot for a sergeant, you had to take on that extra responsibility without even being paid for the privilege.

Callis dismissed the sour thought. Before him stretched the tumbledown roofs and alleys of Squallside, its streets lit by waterproof marrowpitch torches and the strobing flashes of the lightning storm that roared overhead. Far in the distance, rising ominously from the dark waters of the bay, was the Spear of Mallus. The vast monolith of black stone seemed to move closer with every burst of lightning, as if it were some kind of primordial behemoth striding out of the ocean to crush the city of Excelsis underfoot. Callis could glimpse the fulminating energies of the mage towers as they circled the vast rock, siphoning off the deposits of purest prophecy that ran through its augur-touched stone. A flash of lightning illuminated the Consecralium. The forbidding stronghold sat out on a promontory that reached into the surging bay, to the right of the Spear. He glimpsed its soaring, angular battlements and the colossal siege-weapons that littered its walls. The home of the Knights Excelsior, the White Angels. Callis felt a shiver of unease, and turned away.

'A week of this storm,' he said. 'The last thing we need is a flood tearing its way through the Veins. They'd have to send every regiment in the city to stem the riots.'

Custin stared at him, eyes wide with fear. 'Mam lives there,' he said, his voice shaking. 'She'll be okay, won't she?'

Callis grinned, and cuffed the younger guardsman on the shoulder.

'Of course she will, Custin. Don't mind me. If a flood was coming the omens would have shown it by now.'

There was something particularly miserable about an early morning patrol, even when the sky wasn't doing its best to drown you or freeze you to death. The five soldiers squelched through the streets of Squallside towards the harbour, past slick-cobbled lanes lined with stormstone town houses and dimly lit taverns. Here, the housing was built to last. These were imposing, blue-black edifices with steep roofs of grey slate, sacrificing aesthetic appeal for rugged sturdiness. The only warmth that emanated from them was the soft orange-white glow of tallow candles and lanterns through windows and doors. Residents here were well protected from the wretched weather, and the guardsmen could hear peals of good-natured laughter from within the augur-houses, where people came to trade and consume their hard-earned glimmerings. Outside, the vicious downpour had caused the gutters to overflow, and so the dismal conditions were capped by the gruel of rotten tallow and night soil, which seeped into their boots and wafted up their nostrils. Corporal Callis consoled himself by vividly picturing the vicious murder of the absent Sergeant Ames.

Onwards they marched, serenaded by the sound of Guardsman Happer trying to cough up his innards. Callis half considered ordering him back to the bastion, but knew that the old soldier would only bluster and complain about being mollycoddled. They passed through Squallside, and headed down the wide cart lane towards the harbour.

Far ahead they could see the forest of masts poking out of the mist and rain before the sheer face of the Spear. A haze of light radiated from the bay, hundreds of cabin lights and lanterns coating the water in a soft golden glow. No captain was foolish enough to set sail in the middle of all this, especially not upon the treacherous waters of the Coast of Tusks. Tall, broad ironoak and redbark masts marked the great galleys of human captains, gleaming metal chimneys the strange steam-powered contraptions of duardin seadogs. Even now the wolf-ships of the sinister aelf corsairs would be prowling the lanes and edges of the gathered mass. These were sleek and predatory vessels, their hulls festooned with ivory spears and other treasures torn from the hides of the sea-devils and behemoths that plagued the Coast of Tusks. For once they were not hunting. Instead, they watched the flock with a tyrant's eye. No captain would risk breaking the rules of Excelsis harbour with the wolf-ships at their door.

'We'll cut down Rattleshirt Lane,' Callis said. 'Skirt the edge of the Veins, push down towards the harbour.'

There was an awkward pause. Eventually Guardsman Jammud spoke.

'Ah... corporal?' he muttered. 'The sarge doesn't like to go in there. He says there's nothing worth protecting anyway. Just a bunch of pickpockets and knifemen. Why don't we just stick to the trade lanes?'

'That is our assigned patrol,' Callis snapped. 'Besides, in the narrows we'll get some cover from this damned rain.'

No one liked to go into the Veins if they could help it, least of all those who actually lived there. It had been thirty years since the last consecration, since the city borders had been expanded and her walls rebuilt. In that time, the population of Excelsis had almost doubled, with waves of refugees and fortune-seekers of all races appearing from across the realms, drawn by the promise of the city of secrets, where merchants dealt in raw prophecy and even the poorest man could witness a glimmer of his future. With no space left for housing, the city's craftsmen had hit upon a novel solution – keep building regardless. Known as the Veins for its labyrinthine network of cramped alleyways, the poor quarter of the city stretched from the east to the western wall, a rookery of thrown-together, multi-storey shacks piled haphazardly on top of each other with no care for safety or comfort.

'Watch your coinpurses and cover your throats,' grumbled Happer, clutching his steel mace firmly in two hands.

'No band of roof-runners is stupid enough to start a fight with the Coldguard,' said Callis. 'Now get moving. I'd like to climb into a cold, uncomfortable bed at some point in the next week or so.'

Fortunately, the overhanging roofs did indeed provide some cover from the pouring rain, though the streets here were even filthier than the main thoroughfares. There were no drains or sewers here in the sprawl. Wary eyes peered at the guardsmen from behind broken doors and shattered windows, and hunched, pale figures scattered like mice when Custin's lantern shone into the dark corners of the alleyways.

'Through here,' said Custin. Oddly enough, the youth seemed far more comfortable out here on the streets than he ever did amongst the soldiery of the Coldguard Bastion. 'It's a shortcut,' he told Callis, grinning widely despite his soaked longcoat and drowned-rat hair. 'It'll take us out past Hangman's Row.'

'Good work, lad,' the corporal said.

They filed through Custin's shortcut, tramping over the accumulated filth of the Excelsis poor. Fragments of bottles and burnt-out glimmerings, the tell-tale remnants of a drunkard's futile quest for a secret that could get him out of this hell-hole for good – a half-glimpse of a valley festooned with precious amberglass, perhaps, or the location of a swarm of rare quarrelfish. When they were fresh from the mint, the small, silver glimmerings would have flickered and gleamed with the faintest hint of prophetic magic, imbued as they were with fragments of the strange metals found within the Spear of Mallus. Now, their magical properties consumed, they were a dull grey-black and appeared charred, as if they had been sifted out of the ashes of a house fire. Malnourished figures scuttled away into the darkness as the guardsmen approached, like beetles fleeing from underneath an upturned rock.

'What a waste,' said Longholme derisively, her long, oft-broken nose crinkling in disgust. 'You don't get nothing from a few glimmerings. Odd feeling in your guts, maybe. Might get lucky at the card table a couple of times. Nothing you can actually use. Imagine if these gin-wits had saved up all this. Earned themselves a decent living. Typical native-born, can't even...'

She tailed off as Happer dug an elbow into her arm. With an apologetic and fearful expression, she turned to the corporal.

'Ah, what I mean to say, sir,' she stammered. 'Just that some of them...'

Callis allowed himself a few moments of enjoyment from her embarrassed guilt. He was second generation reclaimed himself, descended from the nomadic tribesmen who had flocked to Excelsis when the light of Sigmar had returned to the realms. He had the same dark skin and slight, lithe frame of his mother, a legacy of the many generations his ancestors had spent scratching an existence from the ruthless plains and valleys of the Coast of Tusks. Despite their insistence that all were equal in Sigmar's realm, many pure-blood Azyrites still harboured a mistrust of those descended from the reclaimed tribes. The unspoken assumption was that such folk were untrustworthy somehow, as if their people's long years without the light of Sigmar must surely have left them tainted.

'In all likelihood these lot were born within the city walls same as you, Longholme,' he said. 'And if you think Azyrites don't get augur-haunted, you're deluding yourself. They just tend to frequent cheap brothels rather than back-alley streets.'

There was a chuckle from the patrol.

'Aye, sir,' said Longholme. 'Sorry, sir.'

From an alley to his left, Callis caught a glimpse of a figure staring out at them. It was as pale as snow, and so gaunt that in the darkness it could quite easily be mistaken for a risen corpse. The eyes were the worst. They were swirling pools of ice-blue and white, pupil-less and staring. Not staring sightlessly. It was clear the poor wretch was seeing something. That was the thing about recklessly consuming prophecies – after a while, the world as it was ceased to mean anything to you. You became lost in a world of half-seen, potential futures, lost out of time and uprooted from everything you had once held dear. All that mattered was the next omen, the next secret that you could devour. The figure faded away into darkness, and Callis breathed easily again.

They marched on, quieter now. Any lingering good spirits had been well and truly extinguished by this place. After another hour or so of trudging onwards, they emerged in a small, cramped square, in the centre of which was a bent and broken hand-pump.

Posts, some of iron and some of rotted wood, were scattered around the far edge of the square, and various crumbling porches and balconies overlooked the clearing on all sides. The corporal took a wild guess that the original idea had been for this place to act as a communal well while doubling as a place to hitch beasts of burden. An idea typical of the efficient – or insane – approach that those who had thrown together the Veins seemed to favour. Sigmar alone knew what kind of liquid source that pump would have drawn on.

Two figures stood in the shadow of a rotten, storm-blasted balcony, directly in front of the patrol. Runoff from the slanting roof to their left poured through holes in the sickly green wood, spattering off the hooded and cloaked forms. Beside them sat a two-wheeled dray cart, a canvas thrown over whatever cargo it carried. A rheumy-eyed flathorn was harnessed to the cart, stomping its hind legs irritably and snorting rainwater from its broad snout. Its thick armoured hide glittered as another fork of lightning split the sky above them.

'Evening,' said one of the figures, nodding as the guardsmen began to file past.

In later times, Armand Callis would wonder what made him hold his hand up just then, signalling his men to halt. He would go over this seemingly unremarkable situation, and wonder why it had sent alarm bells ringing in his mind. Perhaps it was the fact that no one in their right mind would be outside that stormy night, not least loitering in the depths of the Veins. Perhaps he heard a tension in the man's voice, a flicker of nerves. All he would ever be certain of was that he made a subconscious choice that would change his life forever.

He approached the pair, his hand resting easily on the hilt of his sabre.

'Hell of a night, eh?' he said.

The nearest figure lifted his hood, revealing a narrow, angular face with high cheekbones and sharp blue eyes. The man smiled, and wiped rainwater from his brow.

'That's the truth,' he said. 'No night to be hauling ale through the narrows, for certain. We're just waiting for the worst to pass.'

Callis nodded. The second figure was leaning against a jutting beam of hardwood, hood still concealing his face. His arms were buried in the pockets of a long, patched coat, and his head was pointed down at the muddy quagmire of the square. Callis quickly flicked his eyes to the balconies and rooftops surrounding them. Not a flicker of movement.

'Don't recall there being any taverns nearby. Where are you headed?' he asked, keeping his tone light and friendly. 'Perhaps we could give you some help?'

'No need,' said the man, waving one hand. 'Stein's doing all the heavy lifting. We're bound for the Hole in the Wall, off Arkhall Lane. It's not such a distance.'

'That's Kofel's place, right?'

There was that smile again, though this time it was masking a flash of irritation. 'Aye, that's the one.'

'Strange, I always thought he brewed his own stuff. Tastes like sewer runoff and nettles, far as I recall.'

'You're mistaken,' said the second figure, stepping out of the shadows, and there was no false bonhomie in his voice. 'We've duardin amberfire here, and it needs getting where it's goin'. If you'll pardon us, now.'

Callis' hand squeezed the hilt of his blade. 'Hold there,' he said, and he spoke the words like he meant them. Behind him there was the sound of sliding steel, and the creak of crossbow winches. 'Happer, Longholme, watch these gentlefolk. Jammud? Check the cart.'

The lanky guardsman crept forward, holding his sword ready

in one hand and a lantern in the other. The two strangers didn't move a muscle. Jammud gently jabbed at the canvas with his blade. There was the clink of something like glass. For a moment, Callis thought that perhaps he had misjudged the situation after all. Then Jammud lifted the cover off, and a wan blue light washed across the pooling water around their feet. In the lantern light, Callis caught a glimpse of row upon row of cylindrical containers, dark blue crystals that pulsed with ghostlight.

'Augur smugglers!' shouted Jammud, his face creased with an excited grin.

The arrow took him in the throat.

Callis felt something colder than the freezing rain clench around his gut. Jammud's eyes widened, and he dropped his sword and lantern, trembling hands reaching for the shaft. He coughed up a gout of blood and slumped backwards into the muddy water.

'Shields!' yelled Callis, dragging his blade free and hauling his pistol from the depths of his overcoat. Another arrow was fired from the roof to their left, and Longholme spat blood, clutching her belly, her crossbow tumbling to the ground. The water was a red river around their feet. The narrow-faced stranger was slamming his fist into Happer's side, and it was only when Callis saw a spray of scarlet that he realised the old man's assailant held a knife. Happer was gasping and groaning, a horrid wet mockery of that familiar cough.

One of the hooded archers crouched on the roofs raised his bow to take a shot, and Callis felt himself move with the swiftness of instinct. His pistol bucked in his hand, and the acrid tang of black powder filled his nostrils. The figure toppled, turning a half-somersault in midair and smashing a rotted hitching post to splinters as he hit the ground, and Callis jammed the pistol back into its holster.

The flathorn screeched and bucked. Arrows were whipping past them from all sides. Callis was dimly aware of Custin at his side, screaming incoherently as bolts rattled against the shield he held overhead.

'Move!' Callis yelled, grabbing a handful of the younger guardsman's cloak and hauling him through the storm of missiles, which came whickering down from above to splash in the bloody swamp beneath their feet. The only way to go was forwards, under the cover of the derelict awning. The pinch-faced, blue-eyed man moved to intercept them, a rapier held at low guard. Callis slashed his sword at head height, forcing the man to stagger backwards, and followed up with a series of low to high thrusts. His opponent easily picked those strikes off, working his feet with the practised ease of a veteran swordsman. Somewhere deep in the rational part of Callis' mind that wasn't overrun by adrenaline and fear, that struck him as odd. This was no back-alley thug.

Custin bellowed and rushed forwards, but the swing of his mace was clumsy and panicked. His shield dropped as he threw himself forward, and the hooded man pirouetted neatly and extended his leading arm. He barely had to put any power behind the strike. Custin's momentum carried him onto the blade, and there was a ghastly rattling sound as a lung was torn open. His killer turned to the corporal, a cold smile on his face.

With a choked cry of mingled rage and sorrow, Callis leapt forward, hacking with the sabre, giving the hooded killer no time to redress and steady himself. The man quick-stepped backwards, splashing through the ankle-high water. His foot caught on a rotting plank, and he stumbled only for a moment. Heart thumping so hard he thought it might burst through his chest, Callis stepped in close, grabbed the rapier blade in one gloved hand and yanked it to the side. The blade dug deep into his flesh, but he held on. His opponent's eyes went wide. Callis punched out with the pommel of his blade, and felt the man's nose crunch.

He staggered, tripped over Custin's prone form and toppled backwards into the water.

Something struck Callis in the shoulder. It tore through the leather strap of his breastplate and punched him to the ground. The air rushed from his lungs, and bloody water seeped into his mouth and nose. He lost his grip on his sword. He felt a pair of rough hands haul him to his feet, and stared into the face of the second hooded figure that had been guarding the cart. The man's hood had fallen back, and Callis saw a broad, pugilist's face, heavy-jawed and marked by a distinct scar that ran from chin to cheek. It was a face he recognised.

'Guardsman… Werrigen,' he gasped.

'You shouldn't have come here, son,' the man he had once called comrade rasped. His face was an unreadable blank. Blood trickled down his brow and he drew a curved dagger back in one fist, ready to strike.

There was a snap-clunk of machinery, and a thick wooden shaft grew from the side of Werrigen's head. The traitor swayed a moment, his hand still pawing at Callis' chest, and then slumped against the corporal. Callis heaved the dead weight free, and spun to see Happer, propped up against the corpse of a fellow guardsman, heavy crossbow held in shaking hands, his belly a ruin of blood and shredded leather.

'Get out of here, Armand,' the old guardsman groaned. 'The cart–'

A hail of bolts rained down from above, spitting Happer from all directions. The old man coughed once, foamy blood spilling into his long beard, and slumped forward. More bolts continued to thwack down into his back, jerking his body unnaturally, like a broken child's toy.

Callis willed his legs into motion, biting back the grief that threatened to drop him to his knees. They were all dead. His men. He had led them to the slaughter. Yet if he did not make it out of this alive, their deaths would never be avenged. The person responsible for whatever they had stumbled on would go free. That was something he could not allow.

Behind him the flathorn was still roaring, pulling against the iron chains that bound it. The beast's great muscles rippled and strained in protest, and foaming drool poured from its armour-plated maw. Callis saw what had the creature in a frenzy. A stray crossbow bolt had hit the beast between its armoured exoskeletal plates, in the soft flesh of its neck.

It was then that Corporal Callis had a particularly bad idea.

He leapt headlong into the cart that the creature was pulling, landing with a crunch amongst shattering crystal vials. An odd, azure mist gathered around his ankles as he rolled through the shards, hauling himself up on the edge of the vehicle, and for a moment he thought he heard a soft chorus of whispers at the edges of his conscience. He fumbled for the pistol at his belt, and fed the shot and powder into the barrel with trembling hands. The rain was pouring down still, and the awning was little cover, but he had no time for care. He cycled the wheel and locked in the cartridge before raising the weapon to take aim at the chain that held the flathorn in place. A crossbow bolt sank into the meat of his thigh, and he howled in pain, almost letting the pistol fall from his hands. With the last of his energy, he slumped against the side of the cart, pressed the pistol against the chain link and pulled the trigger.

By some merciful miracle the powder ignited, and the pistol kicked and roared in his hand. There was a scream of metal, and the chain snapped in two.

The flathorn reared, and took another flurry of bolts meant for Callis in its softer underbelly. Pink foam dripped from its mouth, and it bellowed in agony. Then it kicked its powerful back legs, and barrelled forwards.

Callis lost his grip on the cart rail as the flathorn bolted, and was thrown backwards, head over heels. Crystal crunched beneath him, and he felt hot spikes of agony as shards dug into his unarmoured arms and legs. Yet that was not the worst of it. The azure mist washed over him, enveloping him. He could hear a thousand whispered promises in his skull. Visions followed. Seams of pure ur-gold, entwined about the skeleton of a long-dead magma dragon. A city of a distant realm in flames, its spice mines gutted and scoured. A mother weeping for her dead son. A gleaming knight, singing songs of valour as he slaughtered helpless, screaming townsfolk. Behind it all was laughter, high-pitched and creaking.

Something struck Callis' head, and the visions swam and blurred, a kaleidoscope of worlds and peoples that he had never seen. He was distantly aware of his body being thrown back and forth in the cart, but it was just another dream, and far, far away. The laughter was so loud now. The images began to coalesce, and finally Callis saw something he recognised.

He saw Excelsis. He saw it fall. Consumed by blue flame, the city crumbled. Winged shapes dipped and dived through the smoke-filled ruins of the city's streets, swooping down upon helpless humans to bear them off into the sky. Other forms moved in the shadows. Shapeless, chortling things, delighting in the fear and chaos of dying innocents. Above it all rang the laughter. Suddenly he was hurled across this hellscape of the city that had been his home, past tumbling spires and burning streets. He slammed to earth with a sickening jolt. He was on the roof of an ornate domed structure that dominated the centre of Excelsis. This was the Prophesier's Guild, where the city's valuable stock of secrets was vetted and auctioned. Behind him towered the Guild's great occulum fulgurest, and even now the Collegiate-designed machine was whirling and crackling with storm-siphoned energy. Lightning surged from the six aetheric machines along the city's inner wall, forming a chain of surging fulminations that stretched out towards the sky like a grasping claw. From here he could see the sheer breadth of the devastation. Battle raged in the square beneath him. The ground was shrouded in gun-smoke and ash, yet he could see the proud banners of the Excelsis Guard held high. He could not see what they fought, but he could hear well the screams of dying soldiers, and the fearful cries of men about to break.

The laughter welled up again. He turned. A wizened, crooked man shuffled towards him, leaning on a staff of black iron. As Callis watched, the man threw back his hood with liver-spotted, claw-like hands, exposing a thin, hook-nosed face. He was bald, and his skin was grey and sallow. Long eyebrows, white and thick as eagle feathers, sat above a pair of piercing blue eyes. Those eyes blazed with a furious, reckless joy as Excelsis burned.

The old man raised his staff. The occulum fulgurest whirled ever faster, so violently that it began to creak and groan. Lightning arced down from the great machine, crackling and spitting in protest as it haloed around the head of the old man's staff. With a cackle of joy, the wizard stabbed his weapon down, aiming directly at Callis. The torrent of energy crackled towards him, and the guardsman screamed and held up his arms, knowing it was futile even as he did it. Then he was tumbling through the air, every fibre of his being on fire, until at last he struck something hard and the world around him went mercifully black.

He was lying in a field of petals. Beautiful bottlegreen petals. Odd that they hurt so much, though. Strange that they seemed to be digging into his flesh with such eagerness. Ah, of course, he thought, lifting one stinging hand up before his bleary eyes. A jagged sliver of green crystal pierced his palm. Not petals at all. Callis prised the shard from his hand, and winced as an arc of blood spurted out from the wound it left behind. He had better try to find another field to lie in.

Moving was a mistake. Oh Sigmar, a really terrible mistake. He managed to haul himself to one knee, but then his entire body staged a protest at this fresh violation, and he toppled to the ground, rolling and sliding until he landed with a splash in a pool of foul-smelling water. His many, many wounds screamed for a moment, but the water was cold, and a welcome numbness enveloped him. It also helped to shock some sense back into his battered skull.

The ambush. His escape on the flathorn cart. The visions that did their best to tear apart the inside of his head. He could still hear the laughter of that crooked old daemon rattling around in there.

'What an awful bloody night,' he muttered.

He heard voices echoing through the cramped streets, coming his way. Whoever his assailants were, they weren't about to risk him escaping, especially since he'd identified at least one of them as a fellow soldier. They would hunt him until he was no longer a threat. Until they caught him and added a mortal wound to his growing collection of injuries. He had to move.

Roughly half the cart and all of its contents were scattered across a tight corner lane. There was no sign of the flathorn. Though it seemed unlikely, Callis found himself hoping the creature had managed to find its way out of the slums without injuring itself too badly. It had saved his life after all. Callis himself was currently lying at the side of the road, directly beneath a row of spectacularly decrepit slumhouses built on a haphazard pier and beam foundation. Filthy rainwater had pooled in the crawlspace under these structures, and it was into this brown murk that he had toppled.

As the voices drew closer, Callis slipped deeper into the shadows under the nearest shanty. From here he could see the wrecked cart and the road, and soon enough several pairs of boots appeared.

'Bad crash,' said the first of the new band. 'But no bodies. This is one lucky bastard we're chasing.'

'We're dead,' said another, his voice high-pitched and worried. 'The whole shipment, shattered and broken. Kr–'

'Shut your mouth,' said a third man, and this one was calm and professional. The leader, Callis guessed. 'We speak no names. You, take the road along. The creature's bleeding and half-crazed, so even you should be able to track it. Everyone else, with me. Look for blood, footsteps, anything. He can't have gone far.'

Thank Sigmar for the rain, thought Callis. The downpour had already washed the evidence of his presence from the crash site. He eased himself up and out of the swirling mud that grasped at his knees, and drifted through the waist-deep water. He could see shadows moving towards him through the gaps in the rotten wood foundations.

'Sigmar's teeth,' one of the shadows cursed. 'This was meant to be a simple bit of business. How did it come to this?'

'Someone fouled up,' the man's companion said. A woman's voice, gravelly and slightly nasal, as if its owner was suffering a heavy cold. 'We had the rotations sorted. That old fool Ames was set to lead the outer city patrol, and he'd never have set foot in the Veins. Doubtless the old sot drank himself insensible and left his corporal in charge. Man named Armand Callis. Galtrey recognised him.'

Callis' blood ran cold. Galtrey was the name of a fellow corporal in the Coldguard, a veteran held in high regard. That couldn't be coincidence, surely. This wasn't some isolated case of a single soldier earning outside his wage. This was something bigger, something organised. Sigmar alone knew how high up this went. Not only that, they knew his name. By sunrise the whole damned city might be looking for him.

The first figure splashed closer, idly swatting at the water with a long dirk. He was only a dozen feet from Callis now. The corporal held his breath. He felt a tickle across the back of his neck, and something many-legged and hairy scuttled across his face, inching up past his brow and coming to rest on his scalp. His skin crawled, but he dare not move a muscle, so close were his pursuers.

'Never heard of him,' the man was saying.

'No reason you should have,' replied the woman. 'He's a straight arrow, Galtrey says. Eyes on the career ladder. Doesn't gamble, doesn't earn.'

'Now I really want to gut him.'

The woman sighed, and cursed softly. 'Not today. Wherever our missing corporal is, he ain't here. We could search these piss-reeking alleys for weeks and not find him. Going to have to do this the other way. Let's go.'

The pair turned and waded back towards the street, and Callis waited a few excruciating moments for them to pass out of earshot before swatting at the unwelcome intruder in his hair. It gave a shrill screech as it sailed through the air, splashing into the murk.

He felt nauseous. The accumulated pain and fatigue from his many wounds seemed to all rush in at once then, and it was all the corporal could do to stop himself from sinking face down into the cold, filthy rainwater.

'No,' he whispered to himself.

It wasn't over yet. He needed to ditch his uniform, find somewhere to lay low and get his wounds seen to. Maybe one of the slum hospitals near the harbour. He needed to figure out what it was that he had seen in the mist, and what his next move was. He was not done yet. Whatever this conspiracy was, he was going to find some way to unmask it – or die in the attempt.

Armand Callis turned and staggered through the cold and the filth, away from his traitorous comrades and deeper into the depths of the Veins.

The crooked man's insane laughter followed him.

Hanniver Toll paused, and took a deep lungful of dockside air in through his nose. In rushed the sour reek of dried fish left too long in the sun, the aromatic hint of exotic spices, the tang of fresh-forged metal and the unmistakable stench of thousands of bodies grunting, sweating and hollering their lungs dry as they went about the sacred business of trade. The people of Excelsis ambled through the white whalebone stalls of fishermen and hunters, past garish tents of many colours that promised exotic treasures from distant Qallifae, far-off Hyesca, and a hundred other places, some of which even Toll had not heard of. Ships of all descriptions lined the dockside. Squat, barrel-shaped duardin steam-cogs were anchored alongside swift aelven tide-cutters, the crews shouting boisterous, good-natured insults at each other over the clatter of the market. There were big war galleys, flanks bristling with flame-shot cannon and lance launchers, and even a couple of Scyllan shellships – as Toll looked, one of the giant crustaceans hauled itself clear of the water and into one of the great docking bays, its many-hued, iridescent carapace sliding slowly aside to reveal the crew inside, already securing crates and chests of rare goods. Every captain here would be looking to offload enough of his stock to pay for a nice, reliable augury from the Prophesier's Guild that would lead him to his next haul, and make enough extra to keep his crew paid up and happy. He didn't envy them that particular balancing act.

Toll let his gaze drift across to the stalls. Suspended on great hooks on all sides, dangling limply in a mockery of their former savage ferocity, were aquatic monsters of all descriptions.

Razor-squid, their gaping maws lined with a thousand serrated beaks. Great wyre-sharks, with jaws wide enough to swallow five men whole. Ghyreks, the sabre-toothed mammalian predators that could fly as well as they could swim, so that even out of water a sailor could not escape their vicious fangs. Tall, wiry aelves in leather coats and aprons were gutting and skinning these monsters, or hauling and stringing up fresh specimens for the attention of wandering traders. The acrid stench of the carcasses only added to the stew of potent aromas hereabouts.

'By the God-King,' he said through a wide grin, 'is that not the most beautiful smell that ever blessed your nose, Kazrug?'

The duardin swayed to the side as a cart, piled high with freshly bought goods and drawn by a screeching, two-headed creature with avian features and rows of needle-sharp teeth, nearly crushed him into the mire beneath their feet. Kazrug snapped a sour look back at his companion.

'Stinks of dung and rotten fish,' he snapped. 'And the next fat little human who jostles me will be hauling his goods home with two broken arms. Why'd you drag us here anyhow?'

Toll nodded to a shop-front on their left, a rare refuge from the bustling mass of merchants and dockhands. The two pushed their way through the throng, Kazrug with markedly less restraint. A perfumed, pale-haired merchant wrapped in turquoise robes found himself planted on his backside in a pile of spilt fish guts. He spluttered in outrage as two scrawny servants hauled his not-inconsiderable mass to its feet, but then his eyes found Kazrug's face. He took in the countless gouges and scars that ran from the duardin's broad neck to his single cold, grey eye. His doughy cheeks paled as he saw the chipped blue gemstone that occupied the other socket. And, of course, it was impossible not to notice the gleaming broadaxe that poked its savage head over the duardin's chainmail-armoured shoulder.

'My apologies,' the merchant murmured, a wan smile upon his lips.

'Accepted,' grunted Kazrug, and shouldered his way past.

Toll shook his head and sighed as his stocky companion approached.

'You know, Kazrug, I believe our time working together has proven the efficacy of showing a little restraint at times. Could you try not to antagonise absolutely everybody that crosses our path?'

Kazrug made a harsh barking sound, the nearest he ever came to laughter.

'The job we do, and you're worried about upsetting one pampered stinkwater salesman?'

'It's called perfume,' said Toll, 'and this is the city of secrets. As I have told you a hundred times, everyone in Excelsis is hiding something, and every friendly face could be the one that drives a knife into your back.'

Kazrug rolled his one good eye, and Toll abandoned his planned lecture. He would have to handle the subtlety, but he'd been in enough life or death situations with his foul-tempered companion over the years that he understood the value of having a well-swung duardin axe in his corner.

'In answer to your original question,' he said, 'we are here because last night a patrol of Excelsis guardsmen was found slaughtered in the depths of the Veins.'

Kazrug grunted in something approaching surprise. The odd dead soldier was not uncommon in Excelsis, a city that boasted a number of ruthless criminal gangs amongst its many dangers, but an entire squad? That was unusual.

Toll drew a rolled parchment from his long coat, and unfurled it in front of his companion. Upon it was drawn the face of a young man with a sharp, angular face and hooded eyes. His hair was clipped short in the common manner of the city's soldiery, and he bore a well-managed beard and moustache, curled slightly with wax. Above the image were the words, 'Sought: Corporal Armand Callis of the Coldguard Regiment for the most foul betrayal of his fellow warriors. For murder and theft, and racketeering on a grand scale. Reward for any information leading to his capture – 30,000 glimmerings.'

Kazrug whistled.

'They're not messing about with this boy, are they?' he muttered. 'With a three-count of glimmerings up for the taking he'll be dead in a gutter by sundown. Why are we interested?'

'Guardsman Callis is the only surviving member of this missing squad,' said Toll. 'I've talked to my sources in the Coldguard Bastion, and they say he's a career type, smart and capable enough. Not even a hint of criminal activity prior to this.'

'Were you not just telling me that you can't trust a damned human in this cesspit of a city?'

'I was, and for once I thank you for listening. But I've been doing this long enough to know that something here doesn't add up. Regardless, if Callis is involved in the kind of business that gets four Coldguard soldiers slain, then we need to find him.'

'You think this runs deeper than a black market deal gone wrong?' asked Kazrug.

Toll leaned against the wall of the store, and gazed out across the harbour.

'The city is vulnerable right now,' he said. 'We're still losing patrols out in the wilds. Fortress Abraxicon guards the Realm-gate, and we haven't been able to contact them for a week now. Then a prophecy drops into our laps. A perfect augury. Shows us the orruks of the Shattered Shins gathering, shows us right where Warboss Grukka is camped. And the Stormcasts march to war.'

'This ain't nothing new,' Kazrug shrugged. 'Ain't the first time

Sigmar's boys have marched out to meet a greenskin force that the seers have spotted before time.'

'That's true. But we've had two prominent members of the Prophesier's Guild turn up dead in the last two months. Both of natural causes, sure. Old, frail men. No signs of foul play. Yet now a group of soldiers are found dead.'

Kazrug scratched his beard thoughtfully. 'It's all bits and pieces, though. Not a single thing that ties together.'

'Correct, and in all likelihood I'm just being my usual paranoid self. On the off chance I'm not, however, I'd like to talk to this Armand Callis before the executioner's axe finds him.'

The first thing that Armand Callis noticed was the smell. It was a pungent reek of unwashed bodies and unchecked decay. For just a moment, he thought he was dead, another unnamed corpse dumped in the pauper graves for the endlessly hungry denizens of the earth to drag down and devour.

It was the fact that every square inch of his body ached and burned with agony that dissuaded him of that notion, along with the low murmuring of pained voices. Damp, stinking rags covered his face. He groaned, and pawed at the wrappings with a shaking hand. They parted, and a gleam of daylight speared through to embed itself in his skull. He let out a pitiful moan that sounded less like a man than a wounded beast, and replaced the bandage to blot out the painful brightness.

'Sigmar's Throne, lad,' came a voice from his right. 'They certainly did a number on you, didn't they?'

Callis' hand flicked instinctively to his hip, searching for a blade, but of course there was nothing there. Gritting his teeth, he shifted backwards, feeling a cold stone wall at his back. He propped himself up, ignoring the stabbing knives of pain that tore at his ribs, and tore free the wrappings. He let the light flood in, accepting the agony. If he was to going to die here, he wanted to see it coming. Slowly the corona of searing white light faded, and the room around him coalesced.

It was a typical Excelsis poor-house, a blend of daubed, bleached bone and sun-dried clay, materials that abounded in the Coast of Tusks and made for a cheap yet largely sturdy foundation. Scattered about the floor were beds of woven fibre, upon which lay scores of filthy, moaning figures, all wrapped in rags as he was. Between these stricken wretches drifted figures in white robes, their faces wrapped in handkerchiefs of white cloth, their hands gloved and their heads covered by dark skullcaps. They looked almost wraith-like in the gloom.

'You're currently staying in one of the city's most delightful hospices,' came that voice again. 'A fine establishment indeed, beloved of the lame and the ruined. Cheap beds with fine linen sheets and a host of eager bed-lice whose bites will keep you warm through the long nights. Goodlady Morwen is an acquaintance of mine, and she alerted me as soon as she realised it was our famous errant guardsman who had stumbled into her establishment in the early hours of the morning, two nights past.'

Before Callis was a small, unassuming man, perched lazily on a hardwood stool. He wore an overcoat that seemed a size or two too large for him, dark blue breeches and a pair of worn travelling boots. His face was broad and plain, and the lower half was covered by a thin and scruffy beard perhaps a week or two old. His eyes were a pale grey, and the slightly receding sandy-brown hair atop his head showed glimpses of the same. He was idly rolling a wide-brimmed hat in his hands, but his eyes were fixed upon Callis.

'You've had a busy few days, haven't you guardsman?' he said.

'Are you here to kill me?' Callis rasped. He was shocked by the sound of his own voice. It was the rattling hiss of a man dying from blacklung. 'Normally I'd take offense at that, but frankly with the way I'm feeling, death would come as something of a relief. So get about granting it if you're going to.'

There was a snort of laughter from the other side of his bed, and Callis turned, startled, to see a particularly ugly duardin staring back at him, a grin splitting his craggy, scarred face. The duardin was short one eye, which had been replaced by a chipped blue gemstone, and had a wicked axe slung over one shoulder. All in all, his was not a particularly comforting presence to wake up to.

'He's got stones, this one,' the duardin rumbled.

'I have no wish to see you dead,' the seated man said, his soft voice a harmonious counterpart to his companion. 'But I am interested in how an unremarkable corporal in the Coldguard manages to slay his entire squad, run off into the night, and come to rest in a slum hospital with the majority of his vital organs pulped like a juvafruit salad.'

'You know who I am?'

'I do. Armand Callis, corporal of no particular renown. You have a couple of border skirmishes under your belt, a run-in or two with scattered bands of orruks. You handled yourself well enough, they say.'

'Who are *they*?'

'I also know that your face is up on every wall in the city,' the man continued, ignoring the question. 'They say you slaughtered your fellows and disappeared into the night like the White Reaper himself.'

Callis felt a shiver run down his spine at the mere mention of that name.

The man sighed, and laid his wide-brimmed hat on his lap. He leaned forward, studying Callis with those piercing eyes. There was an unsettling intensity behind the gaze.

'No second-generation reclaimed corporal is worth thirty

33

thousand glimmerings,' he muttered, low but clear enough so that the stricken man heard every word. 'And you don't strike me as the type to slaughter your own men on a whim. Which leads me to wonder – who wants you dead or rotting in jail? And what did you witness that makes you so dangerous to them?'

The image of the wizened sorcerer flashed into Callis' mind, his clawed hands raised and the city ablaze beneath him. He could smell the scorched ruins of what once had been men, and could feel once again the smoke rushing into his lungs and his eyes, burning everything it touched. He hacked and coughed, and he saw the seated man recoil in surprise. Eventually his retching subsided, and he wiped bloody phlegm from his mouth.

'Who are you?' Callis croaked. 'If you were Guild you'd have me in irons or dead already. You're no bounty hunter or findsman. You've no gang markings. Why do you care about any of this?'

'My name is Hanniver Toll,' the man said, rising from his stool. 'I can help you, guardsman, but I need you to tell me everything that happened and everything you saw. Leave nothing out.'

Despite the fact he had no idea who the man was, Callis almost told him everything. It would have been a relief just to get it all out. He almost spoke of the visions that plagued his mind, and the friends he had seen murdered at the hands of Coldguard soldiers. But then he saw old Happer, guts torn out of him, bleeding his last into the rain-slick streets. He saw Longholme and Jammud fall, transfixed by crossbow bolts. And most awful of all he saw Sergeant Werrigen, his face as placid and unconcerned as if he was squashing a bug, as he slid his blade into Custin's chest.

He shook his head. 'I don't know what you're talking about. Now if you're going to stick a knife in me, get on with it.'

Toll sighed as he rose to his feet, putting on his hat as he did so. 'So we choose the hard way. Very well. I wish you the best of luck, citizen Callis. Do give my regards to the headsman. Come

Kazrug, we are obviously not wanted here. Let us leave this man to his supper.' He disdainfully examined his surroundings as he walked purposefully to the door, where he stopped and turned to regard the guardsmen with a final pitying expression. 'Which I'm sure, by the way, will be delightful.'

The duardin stood, hefted his axe and strode off to follow Toll out of the room, caring very little for those delinquents unfortunate enough to be lying in his path. A chorus of groans followed him as he departed.

Two days. Two days he'd been here. Callis sat upright, and groaned as his accumulated bruises and cuts sent a wave of pain through him. He had to get out of here. If some total stranger could find him, the traitors who had slaughtered his patrol certainly would. He swung his feet over the side of the bed, and with gritted teeth hauled himself to his feet. His uniform was nowhere to be seen, which wasn't much of an issue since he'd have to be somewhat more brain-addled than he was to risk wearing it. He was wrapped in a filthy linen robe and breeches, which caused him to resemble one of the faithful pilgrims who made the dangerous trek to Excelsis to visit the Abbey of Remembered Souls. He moved through the beds, past a sea of groaning, stinking bodies. As he moved, he whipped a tattered coat from the floor next to one of the cots, and a pair of ill-smelling sandals from another.

Throwing open the doors, he half expected the sun to reach down and sear his eyes after so long sat in darkness, but instead he was met with a dull, ominous grey haze. The air tingled with the promise of rain and thunder. The storm had clearly not yet passed. Around him the familiar hustle of a day in the Excelsis markets went on, but he could sense the tension and unease in the people of the city. As he turned onto the main thoroughfare toward the harbour stalls, what had once been a fine stone-cobbled road, now almost entirely worn to dust by decades of heavy traffic, a great crack echoed through the street. There were a fair few gasps and muttered prayers from those around him. He looked out towards the origin of the sound, and saw one of the occulum fulgurest apertures on the curve of the harbour wall. The device, one of six placed at equidistant intervals along the perimeter of Excelsis, powered the great lamp-lights that illuminated the bay through some unknowable Collegiate sorcery. Right now it writhed and danced with lightning. A great torrent of energy screamed off into the sky, and Callis heard the rumble of thunder answer it. After a few moments the tumult ceased, but that hardly eased the worried grumbles of the cityfolk. In a city that placed so much faith in omens and auguries, this hardly seemed a promising one.

Callis shook his head, refocusing his thoughts. He had greater problems right now. Where exactly could an errant guardsman, sought after by the very organisation that he had once served, go to ground? He needed somewhere to lay low, reassess his options. But where?

I have absolutely no life outside the Coldguard, he thought. That was a sobering realisation.

The only place he could think to go was to Uncle Tor's house. He hadn't been back there in years. Things had been ugly between them, at the end, but he was sure the old miser would at least listen to what he had to say. Surely?

It was a bad idea. He stood there, as the drifting tide of people swirled around him, and tried to think of a better one.

Uncle Tor Vallen's house was a nondescript little stand-to at the very edge of the Veins. Only a few streets away, the structures descended into the ramshackle jumble of half-collapsed hovels that marked the border of the slums, yet Halfway Lane was surprisingly well maintained, all things considered. Like Uncle Tor, many of the residents here were old soldiers. Sergeants mostly, those that could afford a modest reward for their decades of service once their eyesight failed them or their hands shook too much to hold a blade. There was an order to things here that was missing elsewhere in the modest quarters of the city. Carts were stored neatly in the alleys between the two-storey cottages, which were built of smooth, polished stone rather than traditional bone and clay.

Callis rubbed one hand across his freshly shaved cheeks, wincing as he touched tender skin and the tattered remnants of his once-proud moustache. With his face on half the walls in the city, a visit to a barber had seemed unwise. He had pocketed a gutting knife while a razor-clam salesman's back was turned, and hacked away at his face until it was relatively smooth, aside from the numerous abrasions his amateurish work had left.

Two old fellows leaned against a wooden fence, each filling the air with the spiralling purple smoke of hadja leaf. One was a duardin whose lower leg had been replaced with a metal prosthetic, the other a thin, irritable-looking human clutching a hardwood cane. Both eyed him suspiciously as he passed, for which he could hardly blame them in his current state.

'Good day, sirs,' he attempted, following up the pleasantry with a broad smile that reopened a cut on his cheek and sent a trickle of blood running down his face.

'Hmm,' replied the duardin, and took another drag of his longpipe. The sweet smell, like fresh cut coca plant, sent Callis' stomach rumbling, and he realised how long it had been since he had eaten. Uncle Tor was perhaps the worst cook in the entire city, but Callis would have gladly given his right arm for a bowl of the man's fish head and raw potato broth.

He limped onwards to the far end of the street. Ahead and to the left was Tor's house, an unassuming two-storey structure with a thatched, sloped roof. Smoke billowed from the chimney. A narrow passage separated the building from its immediate neighbour, and Callis ducked in here, attempting to get a glimpse through the kitchen window. It was locked shut, and thick gauze curtains obscured a clutter of pans and plates on the other side, rendered a dull orange by the thick amberglass panes. He saw no movement.

He slumped to the floor outside, and put his head in the palm of his hands. There was a good chance that the traitors hidden amongst the Coldguard had already marked his relatives out as likely points of contact. Tor had been a popular, respected sergeant in his prime, and although that was many years ago now, there were likely still some old-timers who recalled him. That said, he did not recall ever speaking of his uncle. Tor had never approved of his brother marrying into a reclaimed family, and the two never truly reconciled before Adan was killed in battle. Callis' mother Weri passed on only a few years later, struck down by fever. Though Tor had taken the orphaned Callis into his home, he had only done so grudgingly. He had never been cruel, but he had likewise never made a secret of his resentment at having to coddle a child that was a constant reminder of the brother he had never made peace with. When Callis came of age and enlisted he had done so under his mother's family name – a small act of spite that might just help him here. Perhaps that particular familial connection had been overlooked?

In the end, it was exhaustion rather than reason that gave him the courage to approach the heavy oaken door at the front of the house.

It was unlocked. He eased it open, wincing at the creak it unleashed as he did so. Inside the faint, smoky smell of burned food filled the modest entrance hallway. Blades, guns and souvenirs from a score or more years of soldiering covered the rough sandstone walls. There were some new items, too, doubtlessly curios that Tor had picked up on one of his frequent visits to the harbour market: a duardin axe-musket; a pair of Lyndean duelling claws, serrated and hooked; maps, too, and a dozen other esoteric trinkets whose function escaped Callis.

'Uncle?' he said, and the softly spoken words rattled horribly through the empty hall. No answer.

'Uncle Tor?' he attempted again. 'It's Armand. I've got myself in a real mess, uncle. I could really use your help.'

Still nothing. Callis' hand closed around the crude gutting knife tucked into his belt, clutching the bone handle so tightly it hurt. He inched forward. On his left the kitchen door was open. He pressed himself against the wall, drew the knife and shifted it into a fighter's grip, blade running parallel to his arm. He held his breath and spun round into the room.

Uncle Tor sat at the head of the kitchen table, fork still gripped in one hand and a plate full of food in front of him. His craggy, boxer's face was set in a look of mild surprise, and his eyes were fixed on the curved dagger that was thrust straight through his heart.

Callis slumped against the wall. That was it then. Tor had been his last hope, the only person in the city he had left to trust. Grief battled with self-pity in his mind, and he hated himself that the latter won out.

'I'm sorry, uncle,' he muttered. 'This is my fault. I got you caught up in all this madness, and you deserved a better fate.'

'There're worse ways to die,' came a voice from behind him.

Two figures, both in nondescript tunics, breeches and cloaks, with scarves wrapped around their faces. Only their eyes were visible, and Callis saw no pity or anger there, only the detached calm of practised killers. They carried hand crossbows, duardin-forged alley pieces, and he saw the glint of more curved blades upon their belts.

'Drop the blade,' said the first man, gesturing with the hand crossbow. 'And move. Have a seat next to your uncle, if you would.'

Callis did as he was bid, letting his pitiful weapon clatter to the floor and dragging himself across the room. The movement was almost mechanical. He shifted into the only other chair, and tried not to look at the cold, greying thing that had once taken him in, clothed him and fed him. He was dimly aware of the two figures sliding into the kitchen behind him. They were quiet and calm. One leaned against the work surface on the far side of the room, underneath the cluttered window looking out to the street. The orange glow washed across his narrow, angular face. The other, the one who had spoken to him, stood opposite Callis, slid the alley-bow into a leather holster on his belt, and drew his long knife.

'You're dead, guardsman,' he said. 'It's important you understand that. You were dead as soon as you stumbled upon something you were never meant to see.'

He leaned down and let the blade trace a line across the hard wood of the kitchen table. The strange, azure blade was razor keen. The man hardly seemed to be applying any pressure, yet it sliced a deep trail across the worn surface.

'As I say though, there are worse ways to die than a knife to the heart,' the man continued. 'And I'll give you a taste of them. All of them. By the time we're finished with you there'll be nothing much left at all. Just a piece of meat, really.'

He never raised his tone. He sounded bored, if anything. As if he had recited these same words a dozen times today already. Somehow the casual manner with which they were delivered made the words even more chilling than if they had been roared into Callis' face.

'Unless, of course,' the man said, 'you tell us about everyone you've talked to in the last two days. Anyone you may have been foolish enough to confide in before coming here. Take your time, now. Our host here won't mind if we stay a while longer.'

Callis finally looked up. He stared into the man's indifferent grey eyes. From somewhere deep within him, a cold tide of fury roiled up to sear away the guilt and the sorrow.

'I would have,' he said. 'I'd have told you what you wanted to know, if you'd threatened his life. Then I'd have let you gut me and leave me for dead in the street. We weren't close, he and I, but we were family. My life for his, I'd have died content with that. But you made a mistake.'

'You're making one of your own.'

Callis laughed, a bitter, high-pitched noise that sounded hollow in the cramped room. 'Perhaps. But I will tell you this. You've given me *resolve*, friend. And that's a powerful thing for any soldier. So you start cutting. You do your worst. I'll choke on my blood before I tell you a damned thing, you traitorous filth.'

The man snapped forward like a striking viperfish. He grabbed Callis around the throat, and slammed his head down on the table. Callis struggled, but the second man was already on him, slamming a fist into his ribs hard enough to blast the breath from him. The first figure wrenched the scarf from around his mouth, and as Callis looked into his clean-shaven face, he felt another stab of recognition. He had seen this man before as well. He was another Coldguard, a guardsman in Sergeant Volker's platoon, though Callis could not recall his name. How deep was the rot within his regiment?

'We'll start with an eye,' the man snarled. 'Just the one, for now. I'm going to take my time with you.'

The knife came down.

There was an echoing blast from outside, followed by a shrill scream that was abruptly cut off. The blade stopped an inch from Callis' eye.

The two cutthroats looked at each other, then the lead figure nodded to the back of the room. His companion shifted quietly to the far side of the room, knelt and aimed his alley-bow at the kitchen entrance. The first man slugged Callis hard on the temple. His head swam, and black spots burst behind his eyes. He felt himself be hauled up, and felt the curved blade draw a thin line across his throat.

There was a moment of uneasy calm, and then a figure stumbled into view. Another man dressed in simple street clothes, though the drab greys and browns were stained bright scarlet by the blood pouring from a gaping wound in his throat. From the corridor someone planted a boot in the stricken man's back and kicked him to the floor. Ducked behind Callis, the lead assassin shot a bolt from his alley-bow, which clattered into the hallway. The man swiftly racked his weapon with his free hand, sliding the lever back and letting the feeder slide in another bolt from the drum magazine.

'If you're here for the guardsman, you should know that I've a knife held to his throat,' he shouted. 'And more of my men will have heard that shot. You should leave, friend. You won't get a second chance.'

'You're labouring under the delusion that you have any control over this situation,' came a voice from the corridor. It was assured and calm, with an underlying edge of anger. 'And that your backup are still amongst the living. Seven men. Couple of roof-runners that stayed in place a little too long. Few beggars with too-fine clothes.'

'You're bluffing.'

A bag was hurled into the kitchen, the contents clattering across the floor. Seven curved daggers.

The first cutthroat bit back a curse. Callis laughed mirthlessly, ignoring the shock of pain as the blade dug further into the flesh of his throat.

'Kill the wretch,' said the second man. 'We've been made.'

The kitchen window erupted. Pans and shattered glass exploded across the room as something small and heavy hurtled inside, tackling the kneeling bow wielder and sending him sliding across the stone floor. The man holding Callis hesitated just a moment, and the former guardsman snapped his head backwards, hitting his captor's nose with a crunch and sending him stumbling backwards.

Striding into the kitchen, ornate four-barrel pistol in hand, was the same man Callis had encountered at the slum hospice. No longer was he quiet and unassuming. His eyes gleamed with righteous fire, and his stride was sure and purposeful.

'Down,' the newcomer said. Callis dropped. All four barrels of the pistol barked in terrible unison.

The man with the curved knife sailed backwards through the air, his chest a smoking ruin. He struck the old stove and crumpled to the floor, plates and clay cups shattering on the floor about him.

As he lay there panting and feeling the blood trickle from the shallow slice across his throat, Callis looked towards his remaining assailant. The robed figure lay on his back, eyes staring blankly at the ceiling as a thin pool of blood slowly spread across the floor. Upon the man's chest sat the armoured duardin from the hospice, his knuckles bloody and his axe still secured at his back.

'Kazrug, I told you to take him alive,' said the man in the wide-brimmed hat, voice tight with frustration.

'Soft as silt, these boys,' spat the squat, muscled figure. 'But it weren't my right hook that did this, deadly as it is.'

His coarse hands grabbed the dead human's robes and tore them free, exposing the man's chest. Jutting out of the pale flesh was a bloodied spike of blue crystal. It pierced the man's heart, and a steady flow of arterial blood fountained from the neat, surgical wound.

Toll cursed. 'Some kind of failsafe.'

He grasped the crystal, and Callis winced at the sucking sound it made as the man tugged it free. Blood stained the glittering surface of the small shard, which was about the size of a forefinger. Beneath that it was dark blue, almost purple in colour. As Toll lifted it something seemed to swirl within its depths. There was a sound of rustling wind, a sibilant echo that could have been a whisper, and then the crystal shattered into a thousand pieces, covering Toll's heavy leather coat in a patina of fine dust. He frowned in irritation and brushed the stuff down.

'Our enemy is wise enough to cover their tracks. How vexing.'

He turned to Callis, and the smoking pistol was still held ready in his hand.

'Well, corporal,' he said, 'that makes you even more valuable. I warned you what would happen if you did not trust me. I had hoped to dangle you out on the line a little, and catch myself a bigger fish. It seems I must revise my plans somewhat.'

Gone was the friendly demeanour Toll had displayed at the hospital. He studied the corporal with the dispassionate look of a blacksmith inspecting his tools. Callis felt naked under that gaze.

'Who… who are you?' the corporal asked.

'I am the Witch Hunter Hanniver Toll, of the most holy Order of Azyr, and you are going to tell me everything you know.'

Callis felt his felt his blood run cold. Throne of Sigmar, he was in trouble now. The Order had found him. The Order! Stories of their zealous brutality were told in every barrack hall and drinking pit in Excelsis. They were the flame that burned away the heretical and the unfaithful, and the ruthlessness of their methods was legendary. He was, somehow, in even greater trouble than he had been in when he started the day.

'That,' said Toll, 'is the appropriate reaction.'

He leaned down, and those pitiless grey eyes bored into Callis'.

'Every story you've heard is true,' Toll continued. 'Every one. Where we see perfidy and betrayal, the Order excises it with sword and flame. Those that would eat away at the heart of this great civilisation will die screaming. Those that choose to aid such schemes, or who avert their gaze through cowardice or disloyalty will meet a fate no kinder. I tell you this now so you harbour no illusions as to the lengths I will go to protect this city – if you cross me, you are ash and memories, and even those I will seek to eradicate. Do you understand?'

Callis swallowed, which took some effort since his mouth had gone dry. 'I'm no traitor,' he choked out. 'I said nothing because I had already been betrayed. If I had known…'

Toll held up a hand, and like a flash his face was once again genial and dryly amused. All the fury and the conviction drained away like it had never existed. Callis' head was spinning.

'I'm glad we are clear, guardsman,' he said. 'Rest assured, if you do as I say and provide me with everything that I ask for, you need not fear any reprisal. For now, we must move. This place, as you have probably gathered, is far from safe.'

The Witch Hunter gestured, and Callis followed him out of the kitchen and into the hall.

The duardin Kazrug was already at the back door. He had his broad axe held ready in two hands, and two stubby, wide-barrelled pistols were tucked within easy reach at his belt. He smeared blood from his face with one forearm, and nodded at Callis.

'We armin' that one? Might be more than a few of 'em out here.'

Toll favoured Callis with an appraising look for a moment, and then nodded. 'Fetch an alley piece from those dead fools. And find a blade.'

The crunch of broken amberglass came from outside the kitchen window. Toll turned and fired in one smooth motion, and a hooded and scarfed face disappeared in a flash of pink mist.

'Move!' he shouted. 'To the back door.'

They hurtled into the corridor. As they ran, figures appeared in the street to the front of the house, and small iron bolts began to whicker through, skipping off walls and whistling in a storm around them. Callis sent a bolt of his own back in response, and clambered on a cabinet to wrench a basket-handled sabre off its mount on the wall. His uncle's blade, a sergeant's weapon of rank. It was oiled, and the fine steel showed not a hint of rust despite the many nicks and chips along the length. He ran a thumb down the edge, and it came away bloody. Uncle Tor had not been a man to let his tools degrade.

Toll dragged Callis out of the hallway just as another volley of darts smacked into the wall. One tore a line across the Witch Hunter's cheek as it whipped past, but he barely seemed to notice. Then they were hurtling through the back door and out into the side alley behind the house, wedged in between the back wall and a chipped flint partition that obscured the next row of buildings. More hooded figures came at them, brandishing those wicked, curved knives. Kazrug aimed low with a pistol and blasted, finding a kneecap and sending one rushing figure skidding and howling along the cobbles. His fellows slowed as they scrambled over their fallen companion, and Callis dropped another with a bolt to the gut.

'Move,' shouted Toll, emptying the four barrels of his pistol into those figures approaching from the left. More went down, and a mist of smoke and blood wafted down the length of the back alley.

The Witch Hunter ducked, stuck a hand in his coat and withdrew a small, bronze globe. He twisted it and it came apart in his hands like two halves of a juvafruit. He placed each segment in the middle of the flint wall that separated the next row of houses, a hand's width apart.

'What in Sigmar's name are you doing?' shouted Callis. 'They're almost on us!'

Kazrug slammed into his knees and dropped him to the floor, lying on top of him with his pistol braced and aimed down the alley.

'Cover yer ears, lad,' he growled.

Callis cursed and struggled, getting a good nostrilful of the duardin's unholy stench as he did so, and jammed his fingers in his ears. Toll finished his task, drew his rapier and span to the side, impaling an onrushing assailant through the neck. Then he put two fingers to his own ears and crouched low.

There was an ear-shattering explosion, and a column of dust and smoke spiralled into the air. Yet Callis felt no shockwave slam him backwards. He peered into the smoke and saw the ruin of the flint wall. It had blown outwards, and beyond he could see the rear of a house on the next street, and chunks of ruptured stone and flint littering the cobbles.

'Through,' roared Toll, hauling Callis to his feet and staggering into the cloud of dust. Kazrug followed, firing another blast from his pistol and immediately dropping it, letting the weapon dangle from the leather cords that held it to his belt. As they passed through the breach, he flipped his axe back into two hands and waited for the first face to emerge through the smoke. That unfortunate man tasted the fine edge of the brutal weapon, and a head tumbled down onto the broken street. The duardin kicked the stumbling headless torso back through the wall.

'Get back,' said Toll, and stepped up to hurl another object. This was a bright green bottle with a stopper of red wax bound with copper wire. It shattered on the far wall, and for a moment nothing happened. Hooded figures clambered through the gap as the Witch Hunter and his companions scrambled away.

Then there was a sound like a crashing wave, and a sheet of blue flame washed out from the breach, encircling the unfortunate assassins in its path. The force of the blast hurled broken, burning bodies into the house on the far side, and sent yet more sprawling across the floor, screaming piteously as whatever alchemical concoction the bottle had been filled with devoured their flesh.

By the time the flames cleared and the screaming ceased, the companions were half a dozen streets away and still running hard.

Once they were out of sight of their pursuers, it was a simple thing for the trio to disappear amongst the throng of traders and workers that packed the streets of Excelsis during the day. They wove their way through the river of people, past bands of dirty, gaunt-faced pilgrims and bellowing traders, gangs of scarred and marked street toughs, and even the odd gaggle of noble youths indulging a taste for the common life. For once, Callis did not even bother to put a guarding hand over his pockets as the street kids swarmed around their knees, tugging at their sleeves and begging for a glimmering or two. He had nothing left to steal. Eventually they made their way off the main street, and shouldered through the milling crowds and into the depths of the Veins.

'You're a Witch Hunter,' whispered Callis, as the trio slipped down another back alley, a seemingly endless channel that Toll insisted would take them out on the edge of the temple district. 'Can't you just call in some kind of... emergency force or something? Start putting some feet to the flame and get some answers?'

Toll laughed. 'It pleases me that the populace has such a generous estimation of our resources. The large majority of Excelsis' faith militant has joined the Stormcast Eternals on their latest offensive. As for the Order, our ranks are stretched as it is. In every corner of the realm that Sigmar reconquers, a dozen threats raise their heads.'

They walked in silence for a while, wading through the accumulated filth, past mounds of shattered bottles and piles of foul-smelling waste. The walls were close here, and so the alley

made a perfect home for the dreamspinners. Callis stared quea-
sily at the canopy of iridescent webbing overhead, occasionally
catching a glimpse of one of the huge, translucent arachnids
scuttling about its fortress. As he stared at the intricate patterns,
they shifted and kaleidoscoped before his eyes. Colours and shapes
collapsed in on themselves, whirling and reassembling into forms
that promised revelation, if only his mind could interpret them.

Something whacked him hard in the gut, and he doubled over
wheezing.

'Don't stare at the durned things,' Kazrug growled. 'Want to
end up like that one?'

The duardin's stubby hand was pointing at what looked like a
thick, ugly clump of webbing, propped haphazardly against the
alley wall. As Callis peered closer, his stomach lurched. Empty
sockets stared out from the gossamer cage, and a wizened face
screamed in silence, skin leathered and stretched but still recog-
nisably human. As they looked on, needle-thin legs spread out
of the corpse's mouth, and a dagger-shaped body capped with
dozens of glittering eyes levered itself out of its hiding place, and
scuttled with unnerving speed up the side of the wall and out of
sight into the canopy.

'Tell me we're almost out of this place,' said Callis, fighting a
heroic battle with his protesting innards as they squirmed in nau-
seated revulsion.

'We are,' said Toll. 'And don't worry. As long as you're not out
of your skull on brandy or whisper-smoke, you're not likely to fall
under the sway of those things. Keep your head about you, mind.'

Callis shook his head. He had heard about the dangers of the
dark corners of the city, of course he had. Yet it was one thing
to hear rumours about the dreamspinners – how they gathered
omens and auguries up and wove them into those fabulous patterns, how they preyed on unwary drunks, siphoning the hopes

and dreams and worries from their minds and leaving them little more than drooling husks – but it was quite another to see proof of that horror right in front of him.

They were close to the edge of the Veins now, approaching the temple district. Finally Toll lead them out of the narrow alley, and they heard the sound of carts and raised voices. Beyond was a thoroughfare, with the spires of the grand Abbey of Remembered Souls looming ominously in the distance over a row of modest town houses and the swarming heads of dozens of citizens going about their daily business.

'Let's move,' said Toll, but Callis placed a warning hand upon his shoulder.

'Wait,' he said, and pointed down at the far end of the street. A picket line of green-cloaked guardsmen was making its way down the street, stopping cart drovers to rift through their possessions, pulling down the hoods of travellers to peer into their faces, and otherwise making it deadly obvious that they were searching for someone in particular.

'Seven guesses as to who they're looking for,' muttered Callis miserably.

'I have the authority to detain you myself, but I'd rather avoid a confrontation,' said Toll. 'Wait until they're distracted, then we make for the tall building with the shattered sundial on your left.'

It took only a few minutes for the line of guardsmen to become embroiled in a shouting match with a brawny-looking sailor, who was transporting dozens of barrels in a rickety old dray cart. One of the soldiers had jabbed at a barrel with his sword, and a torrent of amber liquid was pouring out into the gutter. A weary-looking sergeant was doing his best to defuse the merchant's anger, and helpfully drawing the attention of everyone in the immediate vicinity.

Toll gestured forward and the three filtered through the crowd, past grumbling merchants and confused townsfolk. Callis nervously clutched at the cowl of his robes as he passed within spitting distance of his old comrades.

On the far side of the street he could see the building the Witch Hunter had indicated, a two-storey ruin of crumbling walls and boarded-up windows. The front door was locked up tight, secured by a thick iron padlock. Toll walked right past it, heading around the side of the structure to another door that was similarly secured. With a brief glance around to check he was unobserved, the Witch Hunter placed one hand on the surface and muttered something under his breath. There was a gentle clicking sound. Toll twisted the padlock and it slid free easily. The door swung open, and he gestured Callis and Kazrug through.

Inside was a sparse, gloomy room with a collection of mouldy pieces of furniture and little else of note. Callis heard the Witch Hunter mutter another unintelligible phrase, and then there was a low grinding sound, and a clank of gears. He turned to see the floor at the north-east corner of the room collapse into a set of stairs, heading down into darkness.

Toll lead them down. As soon as they stepped out into a rough stone corridor, the stairs retracted behind them. The hallway ahead was lit a soft orange by several glowing stones mounted on braziers. There was a sharp, not entirely unpleasant but slightly acrid smell on the air, a chemical tang that nestled at the back of Callis' throat.

'Where in Sigmar's name are we going?' he said.

'Just ahead,' Toll replied. 'You can lose the fearful expression, corporal. No one's about to find us down here.'

The Witch Hunter headed off down the corridor, and after a few hundred yards they came across a pair of heavy wooden doors, which he heaved open. Beyond was a small, low-ceilinged chamber, dominated by a large table that was piled high with scrolls, tomes and a bewildering array of trinkets. Bookshelves covered the walls, interrupted only by glass-fronted cabinets that housed an impressive collection of blades, black powder weapons and sinister-looking devices of a function that Callis could only begin to guess. In the north end of the room was a grand fireplace, above which hung scores of maps and nautical charts of the areas around Excelsis. To the right and left, doors led to adjacent rooms. In the room to the right, Callis saw an intricate array of alembics, crucibles and vases made from scorched green glass. Here, the chemical smell was even stronger, bordering on the unpleasant.

'Welcome to my humble abode,' said Toll, removing his hat and throwing it down on the table. 'Not the most glamorous residence, I grant you, but it suits our purposes for the moment.'

'What happens now?' asked Callis. 'We just stay here?'

'We start with you telling me every single thing that happened the night your patrol was lost in the Veins,' said Toll, motioning for Callis to sit in one of the three chairs near the fireplace. He sat down opposite the indicated chair, and leaned forward with his fingers steepled.

Kazrug took a seat in the corner of the room, where he drew a pitted stone and began whetting the edge of his axe. The scraping sound did little to improve Callis' frayed nerves. Still, as Uncle Tor had been so fond of saying, if you had an arrow in your leg, better to grit your teeth and pull it out than wait for it to fester. He took the proffered seat and closed his eyes, then began to tell the Witch Hunter everything he remembered. He started with the last evening he had spent with his squad, continued through their night time patrol and the ambush in the alleyway, and finished with the apocalyptic vision of the city in flames, shrieking daemons swooping and cavorting in the skies above. Toll listened impassively through it all, not showing a flicker of concern or disbelief, but as Callis got to the robed, wizened figure he had seen in his vision, the Witch Hunter leaned forward suddenly, eyes narrowed with interest.

'This figure,' he said. 'Describe him, everything you noticed. Leave no detail out.'

Callis frowned, and tried to recall.

'He was an ugly old wretch. Bent-backed, so much so that he could barely walk. Hook nose, with a wart the size of a cannon-ball on its side.'

'Anything else?' urged Toll. 'What did he wear? What was he carrying?'

'He was dressed in simple black robes. Had a medallion or something around his neck. And he carried a staff of black iron. The tip of it formed a strange spiral symbol.' Callis shook his head. 'That's everything I remember. I only glimpsed him for a few, short moments.'

Toll sat back in contemplation. There was a long silence, broken only by the metronomic sound of Kazrug whetting his axe.

'You're sure about this?' he asked at last, staring at Callis unblinkingly.

The former corporal nodded. 'Trust me, it's not the sort of thing you forget in a hurry. I'd recognise that face anywhere.'

'I don't know if you would get the chance to,' muttered Toll. 'Archmage Velorius Kryn hasn't been seen in the city for at least ten years.'

'You know who it was I saw?' said Callis, surprised. 'How?'

'Only a mage of the Chamonic discipline bears a staff of black iron such as you described,' said Toll. His brow was furrowed, and for the first time since they had met he seemed genuinely concerned. 'Of the seven such wizards that reside in Excelsis, only Kryn matches your description. He's the most powerful of them by far.'

'Why would he want to see the city burn?' asked Callis. 'What does a Collegiate wizard gain from that?'

'I don't know,' said Toll. 'But this all leads back to the Prophesier's Guild. The shipment of auguries your squad came across in the Veins. The deaths of two prominent guild members in the last few months. And you say that when you saw Kryn in your vision, he was standing before a large cluster of arcane machinery – the largest occulum fulgurest device in the city hangs above the guildhall itself.'

Callis' head was spinning. This had all spiralled wildly out of control. At first he had thought he was mixed up in a simple bit of black market profiteering by bored soldiers. Now they were discussing some sort of conspiracy to strike at the heart of the city.

'If this is as big as you think,' he said, choosing each word carefully, 'then surely it's time to bring in someone else. The entire Excelsis Guard. Maybe even... the White Angels. Someone.'

Toll sighed, and rubbed at his eyes with the palm of his hand.

'The Coldguard, as you well know, Corporal Callis, are one of only three regiments present in Excelsis. The other regiments and the Stormcasts left this city several days ago, in force,' he said. 'The Order of Azyr sent reinforcements alongside them. Flagellant warbands, several of my own associates. We gambled much on the prophecy that gave us the location of the orruks. This was our chance to smash the beasts of the Shattered Shins, perhaps even wipe them out for good.'

Toll rose to his feet, hands on hips, his fists clenching.

'Now I see it,' he continued. 'It was all too perfect. Someone has been pulling our strings all along.'

'There must be something we can do.'

'There is.' The Witch Hunter jabbed a finger towards a wardrobe on the far side of the room. 'You'll find some clothes in there. Get dressed into something respectable.'

'Why, where are we headed?' asked Callis.

'We're going to see an old friend of mine,' said Toll.

ACT TWO

Armand Callis had never once been inside the noble quarter of Excelsis. Rank and file soldiery were not assigned duty within it, with the security demands taken over by ranks of constabulary and the Palatine Guard. Not that there seemed to be much call for arms within the inner wall.

'Where in Sigmar's name is everybody?' he said as they strode down a wide boulevard, the street carved in smooth marble and mounted glowlamps bathing the area in the soothing heat of mid-summer despite the storm raging overhead. 'There's so much... space.'

It wasn't that the streets were broader, but that there were so few people around. Dressed in rich, finely embroidered robes and tunics, the denizens of this paradise strolled unhurriedly, idly chatting with their fellows or stopping to rest on the comfortable pews that lined the pathways. Palanquins that rippled with fine silks of all colours and patterns were carried by painted and perfumed servants. A duardin dressed in purple and sapphire robes ambled past, two servants with gold-painted faces rushing in his wake.

His beard was immaculately shaped into five curled hooks, each tipped with a tiny candle that shone with a blue flame. The duardin stared at Kazrug incredulously as he passed, who responded by clearing his nose as loudly and unpleasantly as possible. The lazy calm of the place sat uncomfortably with Callis. There was none of the shouting, rushing and cursing of merchants trying desperately to get their goods to the best spot before their rivals. In fact, nobody here seemed in the least bit rushed.

They passed by a colossal dome decorated with golden, dancing angels and supported by seven thick marble columns veined with streaks of sky blue. Underneath the towering ceiling were dozens of lounge chairs covered with satin pillows, upon which robed figures reclined like harbour seals, picking at great trays of food and drink. The food was so artfully crafted and colourful that it hardly seemed edible at all to Callis. Crystalline spears of sugar-coated fruit, leaning towers of cake and sweetmeats, geometric arrangements of brightly coloured shapes. Like everything in this place these were works of art to be admired. Lithe, half-naked figures wearing gauze masks wove in and out of the reclining diners, scooping up platters of half-eaten food. Out in the Veins, the waste alone might have kept a family fed for weeks.

They turned onto a wide promenade surrounded on both sides by softly swaying juvafruit trees, their yellow bounty concealed beneath sweeping, white-tipped fronds. Ahead of them loomed their destination.

The Palace of the High Arbiter was like something out of the murals of Azyr that lined the cathedral wall. It was an architectural marvel of the Azyrite form, a wonder of soaring towers and gleaming domes capped with the lightning iconography of the blessed God-King. The great gates leading into the compound bore the engraved image of Saint Rubeus, his blessed warhammer clutched in one bleeding fist, eyes fixed rapturously upon the heavens. From the gates, a pathway of glittering blue marble led to the main dome of the structure. High on the roof above, Callis could see the glimmer of aetheric energy as occulary spheres whirled and spun, a breathtaking mechanical representation of the celestial realm beneath which the city of Sigmar resided.

'Sigmar's teeth,' said Callis softly. Toll thumped him on the upper arm.

'Keep your uncultured mouth closed,' he warned. 'High Arbiter Vermyre's a pious fellow, and he can't abide hearing the God-King's name spoken in vain.'

Guards stepped forward to block their path as they approached, lowering ornate yet imposing halberds. Their armour was so polished and finely crafted that Callis thought they looked less like people than statues brought to life. They wore rich purple tunics and breaches, cream tabards, and greaves, pauldrons and breastplates of shining gold. The surface of their armour was covered with intricate scripture and engravings of the God-King's mythic weapon Ghal Maraz, and their helms were full-faced, with a scale neckguard and a tapered dome that ended in a voluminous white and blue plume.

'Let me do the talking,' said Toll, adjusting his tatty leather overcoat. 'Frankly, we all look like scum, and these upper-city boys tend to despise anyone who wasn't sampling fine Azyrite wine by the time he was teething.'

The leader of the guard came forward. He bore an almost ludicrously ostentatious helm sculpted to represent a star-eagle in flight, and carried an exquisite silver rapier on one hip. He swaggered with the easy poise of someone used to having his every word obeyed.

'This is the palace of the High Arbiter,' he snapped. His voice was plummy and high-pitched, and carried such a pronounced sneer that Callis felt his blood begin to simmer with irritation.

'A reclaimed vagrant like you should have been turned back long before you reached these gates.' The guard took a long look at Callis, taking in the scratches on his face, his ill-fitting clothes, dark skin and hooded grey eyes. 'His grace does not entertain back-alley filth.'

'Just hires them to hold his gates open, eh?' said Callis, before reason could temper his annoyance.

Eagle Helm's plume quivered in outrage, and his hand snapped to the scabbard at his side. Kazrug sniggered audibly, and Toll gave Callis a look that neatly stripped him of the slight satisfaction his remark had temporarily bestowed. The Witch Hunter stepped forward and held one hand up with his symbol of office clutched tightly in the palm.

'Before you draw that blade, son,' he said, 'know that you would be raising steel against a member of the Order of Azyr. That's a good way to get yourself crucified on the walls of the city for the orruks to use as target practice. Now get out of my way before I lose what little remains of my patience, you pompous, blue-blooded cretin.'

There was an uneasy silence, and for a moment Callis thought that Eagle Helm might just draw and start swinging, to hell with the consequences. Fortunately, at that moment an easy-going peal of laughter rippled across the tense scene.

'By the stars, Hanniver,' came an accompanying voice, relaxed and full of cheer. 'I know you have a unique way with people, but that's a bit much even for you.'

'Hello there, Ortam,' said the Witch Hunter, and there was an honest smile upon his face for the first time since Callis had made his acquaintance.

High Arbiter Ortam Vermyre was a small man, and unremarkable considering the astonishing power he wielded in the city of Excelsis. His weak chin and round, slightly boyish face did not resemble the busts of great Azyrite statesmen that lined Providence Way. His robes were of fine silk, but simple and practical in design, far less ostentatious than those Callis had seen worn amongst the populace of the noble quarter. His black hair was cut short, with just the hint of grey at the temples.

'You may stand down, Captain Jaquoir,' said Vermyre, still in that calm, singsong voice. 'This man is known to me. Rather well, as it happens. It's been far too long, Hanniver. Please, come in. You all look as if you could use a glass of strong crystal wine.'

They followed Vermyre down the blue marble path towards the palace. Callis made sure to grace the retreating Jaquoir with his most infuriating smirk as they went, though to his credit the man simply stared back impassively. It was unwise to start making more enemies, considering the position he was in right now, but if there was one thing he could not stand it was a man using his uniform to bully and look down on others. Let the pompous ass glare and seethe.

He snapped back to reality, and watched Toll and Vermyre pull ahead of the group, chatting easily.

'How does he know the High Arbiter so well?' asked Callis.

Kazrug shrugged. 'They go back a way. Never asked about it, but the job we do, it pays to know the lads at the top of the pile. Your man there wields the power of the courts and the constabulary. Even the military, when it comes to it. He's got more power than old Kryn, though of a less flashy kind.'

'Seems like they're friends as much as professional acquaintances,' said Callis.

'Don't know that hunters allow themselves the luxury of friends, but I know he trusts him. And he don't trust many.'

'He trusts you. How long have you known him?'

'Long enough,' said Kazrug. 'I owe him. Don't care to tell you why, but I do. He's a ruthless bastard, they all are, but he did right by me when he had no need to. That debt ain't been repaid yet.'

Callis had no idea how, but a soft summer zephyr rippled across the estate garden as they approached the main hall. It was a strange thing, luxuriating in the refreshing warmth of a summer's day while the sky roared and whirled overhead. To their left he could see the magical spheres set upon the inner wall, their gold and copper surfaces writhing with electrical energy as they drank in the ferocious power of the coming tempest. From here you would hardly know the apocalypse was on you before it was too late. Not for the first time since he had entered the noble district, all the wondrous trappings he had seen lost a little of their appeal. At least down on the docks you knew how things stood.

The great front doors to the main dome yawned open as the group neared, and they entered a cavernous entrance hall. The ceiling stretched high above their heads, and visible upon its surface was a beautiful mural, a depiction of the mighty Hammers of Sigmar Stormhost descending from the heavens on bolts of azure lightning to strike the first blow against the forces of Chaos. It was a vivid piece. Callis felt his heart surge at the sight of the Hammerhand astride his proud dracoth, the wretched minions of the Dark Gods supine and terrified beneath his righteous might. The stories said that Sigmar's champion was still out there in the realms somewhere, leading a band of fellow immortals on an endless crusade against the great enemy. Looking at the diorama, Callis could almost believe it.

'It's a fine piece, is it not?' said Vermyre. 'It's an original Varangino. One of the last great works of his before he died.'

'Varangino, yes,' said Callis, awash with ignorance. 'Tremendous.'

'Come, come,' the High Arbiter said, gesturing them to the left of the dome, down a long corridor lined with portraiture and busts of patricians and warriors whose names meant nothing to Callis. Noble, frowning faces stared down at him, doing nothing to make him feel particularly welcome in this hall of wonders. Even the seemingly mute servants that darted in and out of antechambers and hallways seemed to look upon him and his companions with a kind of curious contempt. Kazrug marched at his side, utterly uncaring as he left a muddy trail across the previously gleaming floor. If Vermyre saw the detritus that the duardin was trailing into his home, he did not seem to mind at all. A pair of irritated-looking servants trailed behind the party like pilot fish, mopping as fast as they could manage.

'We need to talk in private,' Toll was saying. 'I've stumbled upon something, Ortam, and I'm only just getting a sense of the scale of it.'

They entered a long, wide dining chamber, carved from a wood so light it almost looked like bone. Within the surface ran winding streams of amber, swirling and rippling as they caught the light shining through the window to an inner courtyard. Vermyre clicked his fingers, and a servant scurried away, returning moments later with a decanter of violet liquid and a tray of pale blue glasses.

'Please, sit,' said Vermyre, taking a chair himself at the head of the long table. 'Drink. You look as though you could do with a moment's rest.'

He offered a glass to each of them in turn. Toll took one, and so did Callis. Kazrug sniffed the liquid suspiciously, and then shook his head. This drew a vicious look from his employer that the duardin chose to ignore, but if Vermyre was in any way offended he did not let it show.

'What is going on in my city, Hanniver?' the High Arbiter asked. 'What brings a member of the Order of Azyr to my door in such a state?'

'There is a conspiracy amongst the ranks of the city guard,' said Toll. 'And I fear it may reach higher.'

He relayed the chaotic events of the last couple of days as Vermyre listened, grim-faced. When the time came, Callis detailed the contents of his vision as entirely as he could, ending with the appearance of Archmage Kryn and the fall of Excelsis. When the group finished relaying their adventures, there was a lingering silence.

'Kryn,' muttered Vermyre at last. 'I cannot think of anyone who I would like to lock horns with less. The man's a decrepit old wretch, but he wields real power. Power enough to bring about what you say, if this vision of his betrayal is true.'

The High Arbiter clasped his hands together, and rested his chin on them. His sharp eyes flicked back and forth across everyone present.

'We must be cautious,' he said. 'I take it that it is only you three who are aware of exactly what you saw, Corporal Callis?'

'Only us, Vermyre,' said Toll. 'Perhaps the enemy know also, it's hard to tell. Though somehow I think they would have razed half the city looking for us if Kryn knew he had been exposed.'

'Perhaps,' said Vermyre. 'Though it rather depends on how far along this plan of his is. If you're correct in your assumptions, it might be that Kryn sees exposure at this point as inevitable. The truth is, we still don't know what the situation is. Perhaps your friend's vision was corrupted? It has happened before.'

'We cannot take that chance,' said Toll. 'The Stormcasts have already marched into the wilds, taking seven of the ten regiments that garrison this city along with them. Two of my own order march alongside this force, leading faithful warriors from the abbey. We are vulnerable, my friend, and I am short of allies.'

'Then I will move all my pieces on the board,' said Vermyre. 'I control this city, from the courts to the streets, and I refuse to believe that haggard old vulture holds sway over any of my agents. It is time to uncover the truth.'

The High Arbiter stood, and drained the last of his wine. When he first laid eyes upon him Callis had thought Vermyre small and soft, but now he looked anything but. There was a fire of purpose behind his eyes, and not a hint of fear or hesitation about him. He reminded Callis of Toll in that moment, of how the Witch Hunter had looked in the heat of battle, when his mask of calm cynicism fell away and the true warrior of faith was unleashed.

'Wait here, my friends,' Vermyre said. 'I will send missives to my trusted men, and contact the Eldritch Council. The aelves will be needed if we find ourselves in open battle against a turn-coat Collegiate.'

He gave them a brief nod and swept from the room. They heard him bellowing for his servants and personal guard as he moved off down the hallway.

'What exactly happens to me now?' asked Callis. 'I've told you everything I saw. If the city's about to come under attack, I want to be with the Coldguard.'

'In case you've forgotten, most of them want to cut your head off right now,' said Toll. 'Vermyre's got real weight in this city, but it'll take time for him to get the message out that you're innocent. Even then, it's clear your regiment has been infiltrated and cor-rupted. Besides, I thought you wanted your revenge on the man that had your squad killed?'

'You'd offer me that?'

'Son, sending you up against an ancient archmage would be a par-ticularly cruel piece of theatre. I'd fare little better myself. Neither of us will be the one to take Kryn down. But we'll be there when he falls. I'd have thought that would be something you'd like to see.'

The image of the wizard flashed into Callis' mind, of Kryn send-ing down a pillar of searing lightning to murder more loyalist guardsmen. Toll was right. He needed to see this done. For his dead boys. And for Uncle Tor.

'Aye,' he said. 'You're not wrong about that. Some sins have to be answered for.'

'Spoken like a member of the blessed Order,' said the Witch Hunter, and raised his glass.

'Something's wrong,' growled Kazrug. 'Boots in the hall. Lots of 'em.'

Toll was up in a moment, one hand on his repeater pistol and the other on his rapier. Callis followed suit.

'You think they found us?' he asked. 'The assassins from my uncle's house?'

'They didn't march in formation,' said the duardin. His axe was drawn, and he had one of his own pistols in hand. He glanced around the chamber. There were no windows here. Soft glowlights bathed the room in a natural sunlight, and paintings covered the walls.

'Vermyre called for his guard, that's all,' said Toll, though there was an edge of concern in his voice.

The doors slammed open. In rushed the soldiers of the Palatine Guard, resplendent in their purple and gold armour. Their halberds were lowered, and several aimed heavy, hardwood repeater crossbows with top-loading magazines.

'Drop your weapons,' shouted the leader. It was the eagle-helmed captain that Callis had clashed with outside. There was a wide, satisfied smile visible beneath the panoply of his headdress. 'Now!'

'What is this?' growled Toll. 'You are detaining a member of the holy Order. This is treason.'

'No,' came a soft voice from the doorway. 'This is much more than that.'

Ortam Vermyre entered, the Palatine Guard raising their halberds to let their master through as he passed. The High Arbiter's robe was gone, replaced by a tunic of royal blue and a polished gold breastplate. He carried a fine rapier at one hip, and a silver, sapphire-encrusted sceptre shaped to look like a hissing serpent in his hand. He looked more like a general than a politician now.

'Ortam,' breathed the Witch Hunter. 'Tell me this is not true. Tell me.'

'You were always a sharp one, Hanniver,' said the High Arbiter, and Callis could have sworn there was a hint of sadness in his voice. 'They don't see it, your masters. They think you weak simply because you think before you act. Because you wield your power only when you must. I know better.'

'What have you done?' said Toll, shaking his head in despair.

'I have performed my role, as it was ordained,' said Vermyre. 'An old power is rising, my friend, and it is beyond foolish to think this fragile civilisation we have carved out of the mud will be able to stand in its way. I have seen it, Hanniver. The doom that awaits our race if we continue to follow the God-King on his mad crusade into damnation. Only the Dark Gods can offer salvation, and of the profane lords only Great Tzeentch is worthy of our worship.'

'A god of daemons and madness and foul sorcery, who would consume our souls to feed his lust for power.'

Vermyre shook his head. 'I feared that I would not be able to sway you, friend. You are stubborn, more so than anyone I have ever met. But we could achieve so much together. There is a place for you, Hanniver. You need only open your eyes.'

'Was it you?' hissed Callis. He no longer cared about the weapons aimed at his chest. 'Was it you that had my men killed, you bastard?'

Vermyre's eyes barely flicked towards him.

'Indirectly, but yes. War is war, corporal. You led your men into the wrong alley, and you paid the price.'

'They were good men!' shouted Callis.

'I'm sure they were. And now they're dead. If you speak again I'll have your mouth sewn up.'

'All those years, Ort,' said Toll, sagging in his chair. 'After everything we've sacrificed to protect this city? And now you plan to see it burn?'

'Some things are inevitable,' said Vermyre. 'I take no pleasure in this. Yet it must be done. This city was only ever a lie, Hanniver. I have always seen it as it truly is – an illusion of order and law in a universe where no such concepts truly exist.'

'Enough o' this,' shouted Kazrug, brandishing his pistol and axe. 'This one would say anything to get us to drop our weapons. He's a liar and an oathbreaker, Toll. He's been playin' you for a fool for years. Don't–'

Vermyre raised the silver sceptre and muttered a word that turned Callis' blood to ice. A spear of blue flame spat forth from the weapon's serpentine jaws, and rushed forward to sink into Kazrug's chest. The duardin's one good eye widened in shock, then in pain. He sank to his knees.

'No!' Toll shouted, and raised his pistol. He fired straight at Vermyre. The High Arbiter already had his other hand raised, palm out. There was a tinkling sound as four crushed and shattered bullets dropped to the floor.

Kazrug was on the floor, one hand clasped to the horrific burn wound on his chest. Hanniver was there in a moment, but there was little he could do. Callis dropped to his knees and tried to help, but Kazrug's hand batted his away. Vermyre's guards moved to separate them, but the traitorous High Arbiter waved an unconcerned hand to signal them back.

'I'm done,' Kazrug croaked. 'Leave me, Witch Hunter.'

'Thank you for your service, my friend,' said Toll, unable to look at the hideous, blackened wound in the duardin's chest.

'Shh,' gurgled Kazrug. He reached up to grasp the bronze locket around his neck, and tugged on it until the leather bond snapped. 'You take this, you take it home. Give it to my boy. He's got to know, Hanniver, he's got to know.'

'I'll get it to him,' said Toll. 'Rest now.'

'Been quite a ride, ain't it?' Kazrug grinned. 'Wouldn't have had it any... other...'

The duardin's eye lost focus. His hand went slack, and the locket tumbled to the floor. Toll's face was white, his eyes screwed tight. He fumbled for the locket, and held it tight. Callis stared at the dead warrior. He'd barely known the duardin for a day, but it still hurt. Another death. Another betrayal. It was too much.

Toll stood. Opening his eyes, he turned to face Vermyre.

'I want you to know that any friendship we may once have shared is dead,' he whispered, and his voice was as cold as a desert night. 'I want you to know, right here and now, that I will destroy you for this. I will find the things you treasure, and I will burn them to the ground. I will take you apart, piece by piece, until agony and terror are all that is left. Then, and only then, will I allow you to burn. This I promise you.'

Vermyre smiled, sadly. 'I knew it would come to this, old friend. I see the truth, while you close your eyes and pray like a witless child. I pity you.'

The High Arbiter turned, and gestured to his men. 'Seal them in the dungeons, and place a triple guard on their cell. I warn you, if you underestimate this man, he will kill you. I must make the necessary arrangements for what is to come, but I will be back shortly. Then we will find out if these two have been keeping anything else from me.'

The Palatine guardsmen lead them down past cellars filled with vintage wines and spirits, past food larders and servants' quarters. They were deep underneath the palace now. Here, gilded finery had given way to roughly carved tunnels of dark stone, lit by rows of blazing torches. The dungeon itself was a small chamber lit by glow-oil lamps, which housed six separate cells arranged in a hexagonal pattern around a central column and walkway. The soldiers hurled Toll and Callis into adjacent cells. Callis struck the rough stone wall hard, and fell to his knees.

'Before I leave you here, I believe I owe you a small courtesy,' said the guard captain, removing his elaborate helm and stepping towards Callis. Two more of the soldiers grabbed his arms and twisted them behind his back, and the captain slugged him hard in the gut. The air rushed out of Callis' lungs, and the wine he had sampled earlier made a similar break for freedom, splattering across the rough stone floor. Eagle Helm followed up with a vicious one-two combination to his jaw. His head swam, but the soldiers continued to hold him upright.

'This is just a taste,' growled the captain. 'I've seen the Arbiter put the question to his prisoners. It would give you nightmares, boy.'

Callis rolled his tongue around his mouth, feeling a loose tooth. With a snarl, he tore the tooth free, and spat it, along with a mouthful of blood, all over Eagle Helm's breastplate and cloak.

'Bet he hits harder than you, milksop,' he snarled.

Eagle Helm's eyes flashed with outrage, and the last thing that Callis saw was an armoured fist arcing out towards his jaw. When he regained his senses, the former guardsman was lying on the cool floor of his cell. Something burned in his chest, and he guessed that the beating had cracked a rib. He looked around. No sign of any guards.

'Of all my contacts, he was the only one I ever truly trusted,' said Toll, slumped in the cell next to Callis. 'How could you fail to trust someone that has repaid your faith so many times?'

'That was how he got you,' muttered Callis, wincing as he gingerly rubbed his jaw. 'He played the long game, and it worked.'

'And I got Kazrug killed,' the Witch Hunter whispered. 'My foolishness and my trust got us caught. And he paid the price.'

Callis leaned up against the iron bars of the cell. His mouth felt like he'd been gargling cut glass. He sighed.

'You were played,' he said. 'But they made a mistake.'

'And what was that?'

'For Sigmar's sake!' Callis spat. 'They left you alive, didn't they? Aren't you meant to be the man with all the answers? The furious avenger of the God-King, and all that rot? Stop feeling sorry for yourself and get us the hell out of this place. We owe that traitor wretch a further conversation.'

Toll blinked in surprise, then narrowed his eyes. 'You know, even the duardin never spoke to me quite that bluntly.'

'What exactly have I got to lose at this point? Aside from the rest of my teeth, my nails, and various other parts of my anatomy that I'm actually rather fond of?'

Toll stood to test the strength of the bars. Frustrated by his findings, he walked to the cell door and checked the lock.

'No chance of picking this,' he said. 'And the traitors took all my gear. If I had my tools on me I could melt this steel enough to force it open, but that's beside the point.'

They heard boots scuffing on stone and immediately fell silent. Two Palatine guards reappeared to make a quick circuit of the chamber. One of them stopped by Toll's cell and slammed his halberd against the bars.

'Shut your mouths, or you'll regret opening them,' the man growled.

The prisoners waited until the pair circled back out into the corridor. Then Toll began to root through his long coat, searching for anything that had not been confiscated by the guards' thorough patting-down. His hand stopped just above his heart, and his face fell.

'Nothing?' asked Callis, his own heart sinking at the Witch Hunter's expression.

'Something,' muttered Toll. 'Something I'd hoped to avoid using.'

He withdrew a small oval object. It looked almost viscous in his hands, glimmering dully in the soft light of the glow-oil lamps. As Callis watched, the Witch Hunter gently caressed the edge of the object, and it quivered organically.

'What in Sigmar's name is that thing?' said Callis, his stomach squirming in disgust.

'This,' replied Toll, 'is a kraken's eye. It's also a method of direct communication to one of the most dangerous people in the city. And if I use it, I'll be in that person's debt. Which, historically, has never been a good place to be.'

'Worse than being tortured to death by a mad cult leader in his underground dungeon?'

'Potentially. Now quiet. And stand back.'

Toll muttered a word. At least, Callis assumed it was a word, a glottal murmur that sounded like the death rattle of some aquatic monster. Instantly, the organ in the Witch Hunter's hand contracted and pulsed. Black ink poured from the eye, coalescing into a vaguely oval shape, the size of a full-length mirror. Shapes writhed and moved in the depths of that blackness.

'Captain Zenthe,' said Toll, keeping his voice low but clear. Callis winced. If the guards happened to come back now, they were done for.

'Zenthe,' the Witch Hunter repeated. 'I'm calling in my favour. Now answer me, damn you.'

The ink swirled and reshaped, and now a humanoid outline was visible within the mass. Slowly the rippling surface calmed, and the outline came into sharper focus.

A tall, thin creature stood before them, slender in a way that would have spoken of malnourishment in a human, but here promised only lithe agility and strength. She wore a long leather coat embroidered with images of the kraken, with a collar that rose in barbed spikes around her angular face. That face was striking, in the way of aelves, but harsh also, with the hint of a predator's smile. Her hair was short at the sides, almost clipped like a soldier's, and spiked at the tips.

'Hanniver, old friend,' she said. 'Such a pleasure to have you call at this hour.'

So this was the famous Captain Zenthe, thought Callis. The scourge of the Coast of Tusks, and the undisputed ruler of Excelsis Harbour. Tales of the corsair queen were told from Dagger Bay to the Ie'meth Falls and back, and grew in the telling as they went. She who had slaughtered the God of Sharks, and smashed the Sepulchral Fleet at the Strait of Bal-ah-bek. Callis really was mixing in some rarefied social circles these days.

'The pleasure is all mine, Captain Zenthe,' said Hanniver, 'though you'll forgive me if I get straight to the point. My time runs short.'

'Straight to business, then,' the aelf corsair smiled. 'You never take the time to enjoy life, Hanniver. Always lurching from one crisis to the next. How exhausting that must be!'

'Arika, please. You know that I would not call on you unless I was in dire need of aid. The city is infiltrated. As we speak, a cult of the Dark Gods is putting into motion its plan for the destruction of Excelsis.'

Captain Zenthe's soft smile did not entirely leave her lips, but it certainly fell from her eyes. She lifted a goblet to her lips and took a sip, swirling the contents around her mouth thoughtfully.

'What do you expect me to do about it?' she said at last. 'Defending the city is the Excelsis Guard's job, not ours.'

'I cannot trust the soldiery. They are compromised, perhaps at every level. Worse, the High Arbiter has betrayed us. He holds me captive in the dungeons beneath his palace.'

Zenthe laughed. 'That interfering pen-pusher is a traitor? Oh, that's delicious. The pompous bastard has been trying to raise our trade tariffs for years.'

'Well then, you presumably won't have a problem ordering your men to infiltrate this compound, slaughter the guards and break me and my companion free.'

'You want me to launch an assault on the private palace of the city's most powerful and influential figure, all on your say so?'

Toll nodded. 'If you would.'

Captain Zenthe roared with laughter. 'I'll say this about you, Hanniver – you're rarely ever boring. There will be a price for this, you know. This tips the scales in my favour, by some distance too.'

Boots clattered down the hall.

'The guards are coming back,' hissed Callis, leaning out as far as he could to try and get a glimpse of the main door to the dungeon. 'Finish this now.'

'When you hear the screams, that'll be us,' said the aelf corsair. 'Try not to get tortured to death in the meantime, old friend.'

With a wink, the image of Captain Zenthe collapsed in on itself. Hanniver pocketed the kraken's eye just as the guards entered the dungeon. The leader looked about suspiciously, but said nothing.

'Now we wait,' whispered Toll as they turned to leave. 'And we pray that Captain Zenthe wasn't simply humouring me.'

'You think she might not show?'

'Perhaps. Arika Zenthe is many things, but she is no one's fool. She knows that once she plays this card, the only way this ends is if either her or Vermyre ends up in the ground. On the other hand, the captain knows me well, and knows how important it is to stay in the Order's good graces. So I suppose we'll see. In the meantime, there's nothing to do but wait.'

As evening wore on into night, the great glow-oil lamps that bathed the grounds of the High Arbiter's palace began to put out a different kind of light, the warming orange light of midday giving way to the cool glow of a moonlit night. Outside the magically shielded haven of the gardens, the storm raged silently overhead. The Palatine Guard were still on high alert, and patrolled the great ground in groups of three, their fine armour gleaming in the artificial luminescence.

At the grand gate, six armed warriors studied the deathly quiet streets. They appeared outwardly calm, but an experienced observer would have noticed a tension in their movement. The High Arbiter's mask had slipped, and these men knew they played a deadly game – if the Order, or the Dark Gods forbid it, the Stormcasts, were made aware of their perfidy, they would burn for their crimes.

Still, they held their guard proudly. They were professionals, after all.

Six bolts whistled from the darkness. Each struck home, sinking into weak spots in the fine Palatine armour. Six corpses fell to the ground with a clatter.

In their wake came the shadows. They moved as swiftly as wind, covering the open ground to the main gate in mere moments. Wicked curved blades and repeating crossbows glinted in the artificial moonlight as they passed.

Despite their elaborate armour and patrician bearing, the Palatine guardsmen were not just ceremonial troops. They were hand-picked veterans, blue-blooded Azyrites trained in the art of war from youth. They were also strict adherents to the worship of the dark powers, selected specifically by the High Arbiter himself for their vigilance and devotion.

As the shadows flitted across the grand lawn, they wheeled to meet the threat in impressive order, halberds lowered to intercept the charge and legs braced to accept the impact.

Those shadows coalesced into whirling, spinning forms, taller than a man and blessed of a grace that the lesser races could never hope to match. Wicked scimitars smashed halberds aside, forcing open a gap through which graceful bodies danced to leave a ruin of crimson in their wake. To their credit, the Palatine Guard fought hard, falling back to pre-prepared positions, shields raised high to intercept the rain of bolts that pursued them. More than one agile form collapsed to the ground, pierced by a halberd or cut down by a heavy broadsword.

But surprise was on the assailants' side. From all angles came the arrows, and in their wake came the dervishes, dancing in between the clumsy strikes of the human defenders, grinning with the fierce delight of bloodshed as they sliced and carved their prey apart. Like hunting orcas they isolated their targets, fragmenting the tight ranks of the Palatine, creating breaks in the line and exploiting those weaknesses with deadly efficiency.

At the head of the pack was a figure with cropped, white hair, cutlass in one hand and a tri-bladed main gauche in the other. She laughed as she slew, ever dancing out of the reach of the enemy, ever on the edge of calamity yet always in control. Her fencing dagger intercepted sword thrusts and shifted halberds aside, while the cutlass flicked out to open throats and puncture bellies.

In moments, the assailants had cleared the lawn and the entrance hall. Now they filtered through the corridors of the palace like wraiths, crossbows held at the ready.

'Find me the Witch Hunter,' said Captain Arika Zenthe, flicking hot blood from her blade and smiling broadly. It had been far too long since she had let herself have a little fun.

A scream, abruptly cut off, echoed down the hall. Toll and Callis' hosts heard it too. They leapt to their feet, halberds drawn and shields ready.

'We're under attack,' said the younger of the two warriors. 'They're coming this way, and that means they're looking for these two.'

'Finish them,' said his companion. 'Quickly.'

Callis raised his hands. 'Wait! Have you considered taking us hostage? Because I for one would be happy to oblige.'

The younger guard came forward, aiming the spear point of his halberd through the bars. In the confined space, there was little room for the prisoners to avoid being skewered by the polearm.

'We're dead anyway,' said the guard. 'At least I'll see you bleed befo–'

A three-forked dagger grew out of the man's neck. Arterial spray spattered across the dungeon's occupants, and the man went down in a gurgling heap. Callis took a step back in shock, wiping blood from his face. Captain Zenthe stood in the doorway. She snapped him a salute with a bejewelled cutlass, and favoured him with a beaming smile. She was spattered head to toe in gore, and the pale-white of her skin and hair made her look like a banshee.

'Witch!' hissed the surviving guardsman, and rushed forwards with his halberd leading and shield raised. He was fast. Well-drilled. The charge was swift, and the shield was well placed to intercept his opponent's blows. Quick, strong, and accustomed to moving in full plate. To a lightly-armoured defender, such an opponent should have been all but invulnerable.

Zenthe skipped up off the frame of the door, impossibly fast. As the Palatine's spear came in, she planted a foot on the haft, and kicked herself into a forward flip. A perfect rotation brought her down behind the outmatched human, already spinning. The cutlass bit into the man's back, and he gasped in pain. To his credit, the guard managed to tuck in the spear and turn, using the haft as a quarterstaff to try and batter Zenthe to the ground.

The aelf dropped on her back, let the spear rush past her head, wound her body like a spring and kicked straight back up. She scored another wound on the side of the man's neck as she rose.

'For Sigmar's sake, aelf,' shouted Toll, hammering on the cell bars. 'Cease your elaborate dance and finish him!'

Zenthe's laughter was a sinister melody. She dodged two wild stabs of the halberd, and rolled past the guard's shield as he tried to rush her against one of the empty cells. As she came to her feet, she pirouetted with easy grace, slipping behind the bewildered Palatine. There was the unmistakable sound of metal shearing into flesh, and the guard dropped to his knees. Zenthe spun to the side again, letting her momentum slide the cutlass free from her enemy's back. Coughing blood, the guard's eyes lost focus and he slumped forwards with a deafening clatter of metal on stone.

Zenthe stretched like a cat, teeth shining through the blood that covered her face. 'By the black depths, I needed that,' she said.

'You've no idea how dull it is to be anchored in Excelsis harbour, sitting there counting coins with nothing to kill.'

'It's good to see you, Arika,' said the Witch Hunter. 'Though you need not have come yourself.'

'Wouldn't have missed it.' The aelf corsair rummaged around the dead guard's belt, fetching a ring of black iron keys. She stepped over the corpse and opened the cell door.

'Did you find Vermyre?' asked Toll.

'No, worse luck. I was rather looking forward to flaying that fat little traitor alive. His guard are all dead, at least. Along with anyone else we found wandering around these halls.'

'Thank you,' said Toll.

'Didn't do it for free,' said Zenthe, twirling her cutlass with practised ease. She favoured the Witch Hunter with a pointed stare, her thin, dark eyebrows narrowing to dagger points. 'You owe me, human. And rest assured, I'll call in that debt.'

'Aye, I'm sure you will. For now, you need to return to the harbour and prepare your fleet for war.'

Zenthe laughed. 'Me and my crew aren't one of your pet regiments. We're reavers, not soldiers.'

'And what do you think will happen if this city falls to Chaos? This little empire you've carved out for yourself will collapse. Sigmar will burn the Coast of Tusks to cinders before he allows the touch of the Dark Gods to prosper.'

The aelf stooped to wrench her main gauche from the neck of a dead guard.

'I'll have the *Thrice Lucky* beat to quarters,' she said. 'And I'll send the same word throughout my fleet. My people will be ready when the time comes. If you can find some damned Freeguild in this city who haven't turned their cloaks, that is.'

'That can wait. The city has other sworn defenders to call on.'

Zenthe's eyes went wide, and she burst into laughter.

'You're going to parley with that devil? By the bloody-handed god, Hanniver, you're full of surprises.'

'What does that mean?' said Callis. 'Who's she talking about?'

'Refer to me as 'she' again, mortal, and I'll wear your skin as a cloak,' snarled Zenthe.

'You'll see soon enough,' said Toll, and his grim aspect failed to fill Callis with much confidence. 'You're coming along with me.'

Another aelf, face wrapped with a silk scarf, stepped into the room carrying the freed prisoners' gear. Toll took his belt and strapped it on, adjusting the rapier and four-barrelled pistol until they hung loosely at his sides. The corsair held out another belt of faded, cracked leather, held together by a buckle in the shape of a beer mug. Kazrug's pistol was still slung in its holster.

'We found the duardin's corpse upstairs,' Zenthe said. 'We put it to one side. Personally I couldn't stand the filthy little creature, but I know you two worked together for some time.'

Toll's face bore no expression, but he turned the pistol in his hands. It was fine duardin work, rugged and practical, with a smooth wheel-lock mechanism and a twin pair of jagged runes engraved upon the barrel. He flipped the weapon over in his hand and held it out to Callis.

'Here. It's a good piece. Kazrug would have liked to see it used on the people who betrayed him.'

Callis took the weapon. It was heavy, and the grip was clearly designed with a duardin's hand in mind, but the machinework was of the highest quality. He cycled the wheel and checked the hammer. Smooth and clean. Compared to the standard issue gaurdsman's piece, a revelation.

'I'll make good use of it,' he said.

Hanniver Toll nodded. 'Then let's go get ourselves an army.'

* * *

The aelves led them up and out of the dungeons, past a score or more of slaughtered Palatine. Some had fallen to well-placed crossbow bolts, the black-feathered shafts protruding from weak spots in their fine armour. Others had simply been dissected, surrounded and carved apart with surgical precision. Scattered amongst the humans were several aelf corpses. Arrogant blue-bloods they might be, but the High Arbiter's guards had not gone down without a fight.

'You'd have thought that with all this wealth lying about, our dear Master Vermyre could have hired some guards that knew their swords from their backsides,' mused Zenthe.

'He's not counting on a few-score highborn soldiers to take a city,' Toll replied. 'This lot served their purpose. Wherever the traitor is, I'd bet he's gathering his real army.'

The main hall of the palace was no less a slaughtering ground than the dungeon, and as they made their way out into the moonlit grounds they were met with an unsettling silence. There were no bodies at all out here. Just the peaceful hooting of a distant owl, and the constant, low thrum of the building's occularies. It was all a lie, of course. Outside this comforting bubble of peace and quiet, the tempest still raged. Far overhead, beyond the illusion generated by the noble district's aetheric machines, striated forks of lightning tore across the sky.

'We're headed there,' said Toll, gesturing to the east, where the storm was fiercest and most concentrated.

Over the tops of mansions and the distant inner wall, Callis could see a peak of black iron, ringed with jagged crenellations that were silhouetted with each blast of lightning.

'The Consecralium,' he whispered, and he felt a rime of frost wrap itself around his gut. 'The Reaper's fortress.'

'You would seek aid from those butchers?' whispered Zenthe, and the undercurrent of something approaching fear in the unflappable aelf's voice did more to unsettle Callis than anything.

'Once you summon the kraken, Hanniver, there's no safe harbour to flee to.'

'Our hand is forced,' growled the Witch Hunter.

Up close, the great fortress known as the Consecralium was terrifying to behold. Like most of the mortal inhabitants of Excelsis, Callis did his best to put its existence out of his mind. It was always there of course, looming in the distance through the morning mists like an executioner's axe hanging over the head of every single person in the city. Yet if you didn't look at it, if you ignored the storms that raged daily over its black iron battlements, you could almost forget the stories. The tall tales of the slaughter enacted at the height of the purges, and worse, the haunted truths told by those old-timers who had been lucky enough to survive when the full fury of the White Angels had been unleashed.

They strode across the great bridge to the fortress, the rain whipping at them and the wind surging against them as if anxious to dissuade them from their course. Ahead was a door tall enough for a gargant and wide enough for a ship, every inch engraved with images that could not be picked out in the downpour. What Callis could see were the murder-holes spread out across the face of the structure, great dark portals from which protruded the snouts of colossal ballistae, ranged and aimed to hurl their deadly missiles down upon the bridge and anyone foolish enough to attempt to cross it without permission. He was uncomfortably aware that he currently qualified as such a target.

Several dozen yards from the gatehouse they came to a halt. The battlements soared so high above them that Callis had to lean back to glimpse the teeth of the crenellations. He felt utterly, totally insignificant. Even the rugged might of the guard bastions were as nothing compared to the unthinkable dimensions of this place. The very idea of any army attacking a city that held such a structure seemed almost laughable.

Hanniver Toll stepped forward, removing his wide-brimmed hat. The wind and rain whipped his hair back and forth, and he raised his cold, grey eyes to the sky.

'Here stands Witch Hunter Hanniver Toll, of the hallowed Order of Azyr,' he bellowed. 'The city is in grave danger. Lord of the tower, come forth. In Sigmar's name, come forth!'

Even through the storm, his words carried strongly.

All that could be heard was the roar and screech of the wind as it whipped past them, and the cracking in the skies above. They waited there. By now the rain had seeped into every inch of Callis' clothing, and his body was numb with the freezing cold. His hand was still nervously wrapped around the hilt of his sword, but he could not feel the comforting grooves of the metal. Toll, several steps ahead, did not move a muscle. He wasn't even shaking with the cold.

After what seemed like an eternity, the ground began to rumble beneath their feet. A sound like a galleon being carved open upon the reef met their ears, and, with aching slowness, the grand doors of the Consecralium began to inch open. Beyond, all was darkness, though Callis thought he saw the briefest glimpse of a flickering blue light. No formation of soldiers marched out of those doors. Only a single figure. And he was enough to very nearly bring Armand Callis to his knees.

As a guardsman he had seen the warriors of Sigmar every now and then, marching in perfect order in their full battle array, gods of war sent down amongst mere mortals. It was always from a distance, though. In his six years of service, Callis had never stood so close to one of these peerless, mythic warriors. And as this champion neared, it was clear that he was an exemplar even amongst his own kind. His armour was pristine white, so polished and perfect that it gleamed in the storm like a beacon. It was fabulously ornate, so beautifully made that it seemed impossible that mortal hands had crafted it. Perhaps they had not. A cape of azure blue swirled around the figure's shoulders, and his battle-mask was a pitiless white visage crested by a golden vision of an exploding sun. One hand rested on the hilt of a broadsword large enough to carve a troggoth in two, while the other held a staff upon which hung a golden lantern.

Yet it was none of these wondrous items that made this giant extraordinary. It was the aura that resonated from him. Callis felt every layer of his soul being stripped away under the expressionless gaze of that white mask. Every sin he had ever committed, every black thought he had ever entertained, rippled to the surface of his mind. There was no hiding from this. There was no man or woman alive that could hold on to a lie in the face of such pure and radiant truth. Callis wanted to fall to his knees, confess every mortal weakness he had ever allowed himself to partake in.

'Hold your nerve,' said Toll. Callis spared a glance at the man. His jaw was set, and if he felt any fear or uncertainty he did not let it show. The Witch Hunter's expression had hardly changed since Kazrug had been slain. His eyes burned with furious purpose, the gaze of a man who would pay any price to gain his revenge.

The figure stopped a few yards from them. He stared at each of them in turn, but said nothing. After several tense moments that seemed to stretch on for hours, Toll ventured to break the silence.

'Lord Sentanus,' he said. Callis felt his skin crawl at the mention of that name.

Lord-Veritant Cerrus Sentanus. The White Reaper. The saint of the purge. Amongst the many monsters and bogeymen that the parents of Excelsis invoked to send their unruly children to sleep, the figure that inspired the most terror was one of the city's most famous warriors. The inquisitor-lord of the Knights Excelsior. The pitiless, ruthless executioner of the lost and the damned.

'Speak,' the war god rasped. His voice was the sound of thunder.

The sound of an avalanche. Of an ice-shelf collapsing. Yet despite all its power, there was a faintly human edge of impatience to it.

Toll stepped forwards, holding up the symbol of his order.

'There is a conspiracy within the city,' he said, and his voice did not tremble for an instant. 'A cult of the Dark Gods has embedded itself throughout the hierarchy. The High Arbiter is one of them. As is the archmage Velorius Kryn. They have agents within the Excelsis Guard, and certainly the Prophesier's Guild.'

The Reaper continued to stare at Toll, not moving a muscle. He was so still it seemed as if he had been frozen in time.

'You have seen the High Arbiter's perfidy first-hand,' he said at last. 'What of Kryn?'

'This man was a corporal in the city guard,' said the Witch Hunter, indicating Callis. 'While on patrol, he stumbled upon what appeared to be a black market trade of illicit auguries. There was an ambush. As he escaped, he was exposed to the stolen prophecies, and saw a vision of the city in ruins, burned to cinders by the archmage's hands.'

The towering warrior turned to regard Callis for the first time. 'Come forward,' said the Reaper.

Callis' feet moved, though whether under his own volition or simply by virtue of the command, he did not know. His heart hammered in the frozen pit of his chest, and he trembled as if fever-sick.

The Reaper raised his lantern-staff and Callis cowered, expecting to be blasted into a million bloody fragments. Instead, the front of the device opened and radiant light poured forth, a searing ray of brilliant luminescence that bored into every fibre of his being. There was no hiding from this blinding radiance. It was the omniscience of gods, the indefatigability of pure truth. Callis fell to his knees. He had never thought of himself as a bad man. But in the face of that light he knew that he was guilty. Guilty of a thousand careless, senseless mortal weaknesses. Petty, hateful acts. Moments of cruelty and vice that he had excused or conveniently forgotten. Taken together, they were more than reason enough for this avatar of pitiless judgment to scour his very presence from the world. The light took everything. It pried loose every secret he held dear. Not just the truth of the visions, but older, harder secrets buried so deep within him that he had almost forgotten their power. The silhouette of his father in the fading light as he walked away to battle for the last time. Knives in the alleyways, as a wayward, angry youth. The terrified, pain-wracked face of the first man he had ever killed.

'Stop,' he gasped.

The cry of grief from his mother when she found out her husband would never return.

'Please, stop!'

The light cut out. Somehow the freezing lash of the rain was a blessed relief.

'You saw what you needed to?' came Toll's voice. There was no concern or pity there. All business.

The Reaper's expressionless mask remained fixed on Callis. He felt those eyes boring into him as a physical ache. Any moment now, the killing blow would come, he knew. He closed his eyes, and waited for the bite of the sword upon his neck.

'Lord-Veritant Sentanus,' said the Witch Hunter, 'I still have need of this one. His foresight may be invaluable in the battle to come. In the name of the Order, I must claim him.'

Slowly, the Reaper's head turned to fix his eyes on Toll. Callis risked a look up. Somehow Toll did not falter under that scrutiny. He stood tall amidst the storm that whipped at his long coat and hair, returning the Stormcast's gaze in kind.

'You have no authority here, mortal,' said Sentanus. 'Remember that.'

With that he turned and strode away, back towards the fortress.

'Wait!' shouted Toll. 'You would walk away? The city will fall if we do nothing!'

His words drifted away on the wind. The Reaper disappeared into the depths of the Consecralium, and moments later the great doors began to slide closed once more. Then they were alone. Neither said anything for a while. Callis knelt in the rain, trying vainly to regather his wits. It was like letting the world bleed back in after a heavy night's drinking. His skull throbbed, and trying to hold on to a thought was like grasping a handful of mist. All he could see was the searing light, framing that pitiless mask of judgement.

'Well,' he said, after what seemed like several minutes. 'I don't think that was as successful as we hoped. I, for one, feel bloody awful. Like someone's taken an axe to my skull.'

'They very nearly did,' muttered Toll. His brows were furrowed in concern.

'Where do we go from here?' asked Callis. 'If the Stormcasts won't help us, who will?'

Toll thought for a moment. 'You told me that in your vision you saw loyalist warriors fighting back against the invaders,' he said.

'Yes. They were dying in droves, but they still held the city centre. Until the archmage decided to drop a lightning storm on them, anyway.'

'Did you see any heraldry? Which regiments fought for the city?'

Callis closed his eyes, tried to picture the fall of Excelsis. It was hazy now, like a half-remembered nightmare. He saw the square alight, under the glare of the arcane machinery of the Prophesier's Guild. He saw the flocks of shrieking shadows flitting through the smoke-filled streets. There was the cluster of battered companies, still holding a semblance of order despite the corpses that lined the cobbles. Their banners were raised, charred and tattered, but still defiant in the face of obliteration.

'The Iron Bull of Tarsus,' Callis said. 'That's the symbol of the Eighth, under General Synor.'

'Tell me of him.'

'Well, he's...'

'You're not in the Freeguild any more, Armand.'

'He's an old soldier gone to fat, who prefers brandy and pipe-spice to getting his hands dirty. He's had his glories in the past, but his Iron Bulls took a hell of a hammering when the orruks last raided the Realmgate. Since then they've been on regular garrison duty, along with the Coldguard and the Firewolves, while the remaining regiments support the Stormcasts' offensive along the coast.'

Toll nodded, and began to march back the way they had come, towards the city. Callis followed. As he walked he glanced out over the plains. Spears of faint light had already begun to appear over the distant hills.

'We're running out of time,' muttered the Witch Hunter. 'I know Vermyre. He would never have revealed himself if he wasn't certain of his position. As we speak he'll be moving his pieces across the board, ready to unleash the killing blow. I only hope we can alert the city garrison in time.'

The Iron Bulls' bastion was bustling with activity. Flathorns and other cart-beasts hauled ammunition and supplies to and fro, whinnying and snorting their complaints at their short-tempered drovers. In the great yard before the entrance, a batch of new recruits were being beaten into shape to the chorus of a dozen bellowing drill sergeants.

'You know, that reward is still on my head,' muttered Callis, doing his level best to try and shrink into his collar. 'Typically it's a bad idea for fugitives to wander right into their pursuers' camp.'

'Most fugitives aren't accompanied by a member of the Order Azyr,' said Toll. 'The general has no choice but to hear me, unless he wishes to start a internecine war with the faithful. If what you told me about him is true, that seems unlikely.'

This place was bigger than the Coldguard Bastion by some measure. The great face of the edifice loomed before them, an imposing, if blunt, example of duardin stonecraft bristling with murder-holes, flame cannons and balconies guarded by green-coated defenders. It was a mere fraction of the artillery power that faced out into the wilds, but the defenders of Excelsis had long ago learned that high walls were not always a sure defence against a determined enemy. Abutted against the fortress wall were several large, low-roofed buildings with great iron doors. One was hauled open to admit one of the supply carts, and Callis caught a glimpse of row upon row of cannon barrels. Clearly the Iron Bulls did not lack for field pieces.

As they made their way towards the great gate, a squad of halberdiers moved to block their way.

'Your business here?' asked the sergeant, with the casual boredom of someone who had been on guard duty a few hours too long.

'My own,' said Toll, holding out his symbol of office and not even bothering to slow his pace.

The sergeant paled.

'Of... of course, sire,' he mumbled. Then his eyes met Callis' and widened in surprise. He levelled his halberd. 'You! Men, detain this traitor.'

Suddenly Callis was surrounded with a wall of steel, prodding uncomfortably close to his throat. He raised his hands, very, very slowly.

'The corporal is with me,' said Toll.

'This piece of scum killed his own men. Four dead men and women, betrayed by their officer. I don't care if you're the White Reaper himself, he's for the dungeons.'

Toll stepped close to the sergeant. When he spoke, his voice was low, calm, and icy cold.

'Sergeant, this man is guilty of no crime. You, however, are just now on the verge of committing one of your own. Do you know the penalty for obstructing a member of the Holy Order in the course of his duties?'

There was a crowd now. Callis was uncomfortably aware of the number of heavily armed men and women in the immediate vicinity who would have like nothing less than to see his head on a spike adorning the city walls. The courtyard was deathly quiet.

'I am here to speak with General Synor,' said Toll. 'And this man is still of use to me. If you delay me further, you put the people of this city in danger. And you forfeit your own life.'

The Witch Hunter's hand dropped to his belt, brushing his coat aside to reveal his four-barrelled pistol. The sergeant's eyes flicked to the weapon, and back to Callis. Slowly, he withdrew his halberd, and his soldiers followed suit. The air was still thick with tension. Storm clouds rumbled overhead.

'If you want to see the general, you'll go under armed guard,' the sergeant said. He signalled to several burly guardsmen armed with handguns that were currently pointed at the intruders. They moved to surround Callis and Toll, weapons lowered and ready to shoot. Callis felt a sick sense of vulnerability – if even one of these men was a traitor, his guts could be spattered all over the fortress walls in less time than it took to blink.

'If they make the slightest false move, shoot them,' said the sergeant.

General Synor's quarters were at the very summit of the bastion, hidden amongst a network of corridors. Here, the walls were decorated with busts and portraits of deceased Freeguild heroes, and soldiers dressed in fine silver breastplates and immaculate white tunics stood at guard. These were the general's personal retinue, chosen from amongst the most experienced and skilled soldiers in the regiment. They did not even risk a glance up as the retinue strode past. When they reached the end of a long hallway carpeted in rich scarlet and flanked by statues of Stormcast warriors raising their warhammers defiantly at some unseen foe, the officer leading them bade them wait. Callis was pacing interminably, face locked in a troubled frown. Toll found the man's refusal to stand still deeply irritating, but said nothing. He understood that feeling of anxious helplessness better than most.

Finally, after what seemed like an age, the door at the end of the corridor swung open, and the officer gestured them through.

The smell of spice-smoke hit Toll like an open hand as soon as he entered the room. He'd never developed a taste for the stuff. Partly due to its acrid, chemical tang, but also because the arraca plant from which it came lay far outside the city walls, and even with the auguries to guide their way, the death toll for those who harvested it could be described as horrific.

General Synor sat in a luxuriously padded chair, slightly obscured amidst a cloud of smoke, a blazing spice-pipe propped lazily between his lips. He rose as they entered, and raised a fist to his chest in salute.

'Greetings,' he said, and his voice was the low, gravelly rumble of a man who had replaced sleep with liquor and spice over the last few days.

Toll raised a fist to his chest in salute, letting an appraising eye drift across the general. The man was rapidly leaving middle age behind, and though he wasn't in terrible shape there was a hint of roundness to his belly that spoke of a sedentary lifestyle and a soldier who'd been away from the frontline for too long. His hair was black with a hint of grey, a simple crop that trailed into two impressive muttonchops and a well-maintained beard. He wore a look of bored frustration.

'Not often we host one of the Order here at the Bastion,' he drawled. 'Much less in the company of a wanted criminal. I suppose you have a good reason for me not to immediately throw this murderer in the dungeons?'

Callis looked as if he were about to say something, but thankfully decided to keep his mouth shut. Miracles did happen. In truth, the man had looked pale and drawn ever since they had left the bridge of the Consecralium.

'Corporal Callis is innocent,' Toll said. 'That's part of the reason why I'm here. His regiment, the Coldguard, has been fatally compromised by a faction of heretic cultists. We do not know how far this rot has spread through Excelsis' military. It may be that even your own regiment is corrupted.'

Synor snorted. 'The Iron Bulls have been stalwart faithful of Sigmar since the Wars of Founding, when we took the colour of the Excelsis city guard,' he said. 'Every tenday the priests arrive to renew our vows of loyalty and sanctify our guns. This sounds to me like nothing more than the desperate excuses of a man who realises he's for the executioner's axe.'

'I have seen the conspiracy firsthand,' Toll continued. 'And it reaches beyond the military. The High Arbiter himself has turned his cloak. I come here fresh from a stay in the dungeons of the Arbiter's palace. The archmage Velorius Kryn is also implicated. Together they are planning some form of attack on the city. Perhaps even an armed uprising.'

The general's eyes widened at that. He said nothing for a moment, instead simply staring straight at the Witch Hunter. Toll knew the man was sorting through the mess that had just been dumped on his desk. On the one hand, the idea of the High Arbiter of all people betraying the city was patently ludicrous. On the other, one tended not to doubt the word of a member of the Order of Azyr.

'If Vermyre has betrayed us, where is he now?' Synor said. 'What is his objective? Perhaps he has spies inside the city guard, but surely not enough to take the damned city.'

'I don't know yet. But I do know Vermyre, and he's man who always has a plan. We need to be ready. The army needs to take to the streets, in force. We must secure the Prophesier's Guild and the main square. It is likely that whatever Kryn and the High Arbiter have planned, it will involve the Guild.'

'Wait,' said Synor, rubbing furiously at the bridge of his nose, his eyes squeezed tightly shut. 'Wait. You want me to march on Collegiate territory? With no proof of anything but your rogue guardsman's word?'

'My proof is my profession, general,' said Toll, fixing the man with the look he used to signal he was no longer interested in playing games. 'You know the consequences for obstructing a member of the Order in his duties.'

Toll realised immediately that he had made a mistake.

Synor's eyes narrowed, and his cheeks flushed red with anger. 'You dare to come here with your half-baked theories and threaten me?' he snarled. 'I am a general in Sigmar's holy army, you arrogant thug. Not some pimple-faced guardsman you can push around.'

Toll cursed his impatience. *Never underestimate the pride of a powerful man,* he thought. Technically he had authority here, but Freeguild officers always chafed at being ordered around by what they saw as little more than jumped-up civilians. He should have played this more carefully. He summoned up the last reserves of his patience and tried again.

'General, I assure you that the situation is grave enough to warrant such action. I would not have spoken so bluntly otherwise.'

There was a crack of lightning. The brief respite had ended, and once more the sky outside broiled with dark clouds. Rain thrashed against the windows. Synor sat down, put down his spice-pipe and fixed the Witch Hunter with an imperious glare.

'I am in control of this city's defences,' he said, emphasising every word as if he was talking to a fool. 'Which are already stretched thin by the sortie against the orruks. Seven entire regiments marched alongside the Stormcasts; the Revenant Spears, the Bronze Claws, the Stormblessed and all the rest. I have but three remaining to safeguard a city of hundreds of thousands. I will not charge off on some damned fool errand on the word of a wanted criminal.'

Sergeant Steerman was as relaxed as he had been in months. Which was to say, there weren't currently any greenskin savages howling their blood-curdling war cries at him, and he was pleasantly bored rather than desperate and terrified. Yes, he could stand for a few more days on guard duty. Let those pompous fools in the Stormblessed run around chasing orruks and medals. The Firewolves would do the unglamorous work of keeping the city safe, and Steerman would enjoy this pleasant boredom.

From his position on the outer wall he could see out across the Blooded Field, the stretch of rough land ahead of the city walls which had played host to a hundred different warbands and brutal hordes set on tearing down this monument to order and civilization. Without thousands of leering orruk faces or the bloodstained idols of degenerate tribesmen, the low, broken hills and windswept plains ahead of him were almost ruggedly beautiful, Steerman thought. Or they would be, if it were not for the ever-present storm clouds. As he gazed out, another fork of lightning flickered across the landscape, and a moment later there was a deep rumble. Steerman sighed, and glanced up at the bruised canvas of sky above him. This damned storm was going nowhere soon.

'Sir,' said Guardsman Collick, snapping the sergeant out of his daydreaming. 'There's another patrol approaching.'

That was odd. As far as Steerman knew there weren't supposed to be any changeovers for several hours yet. He stood, made his way out of the guard tower and peered down the length of the wall. There were indeed a number of figures headed this way. There was a deafening crack and a flash of lightning, which almost made him jump out of his boots. The damned occulum had been playing up all morning. He turned to gaze up at the whirling brass orb, which rippled with arcs of blue-white energy. There was a constant low hum in the air that set his teeth on edge a little, but that was a small price to pay for this extended rest.

He checked his sword belt was secure – on the off chance there was a ranking officer in this mob – and strode off towards the newcomers.

The leader was a small fellow with a sergeant's stripes, a wiry specimen with darting blue eyes and dirty blonde hair. He smiled as he approached. Steerman didn't recognise him, but that wasn't too surprising. His lot had been out in the field a long time. He snapped off a quick salute.

'Morning lads,' he said.

'Sergeant Steerman, right? My name's Arvine,' said the new-comer, returning with a salute of his own. His eyes were fixed on the crackling light-engines. Steerman grinned.

'Don't worry, friend. They're on the turn today, but there's no danger. They're not about to go haywire and destroy the city.'

Arvine turned his blue eyes turned back to Steerman with the oddest expression on his face, halfway between a smile and a grimace. Steerman noticed that the man's nose was crooked and freshly bruised. Doubtless the result of a harmless barrack-hall scrap of some sort. He chose not to mention it. The newcomer walked closer, reaching into his jacket.

'We're to relieve you,' he said. 'General Revard's orders.'

Steerman furrowed his brows in confusion. 'How's that then? What's the use in swapping us with another squad?'

'You're relieved, sergeant,' said the newcomer, and he drew a parchment scroll from the lining of his jacket. Steerman thought it was a copy of the orders at first, but then he saw the eight-pointed star scrawled across the surface. He saw other symbols, too, that flooded his mouth with bile and sent his head to spinning. Arvine was smiling. Steerman reached a trembling hand to his side, fumbling for his blade.

The man in the sergeant's uniform spoke three words.

Steerman saw a flash of blue light and felt a wave of heat strike him in the chest, and then he was soaring backwards, limbs flailing uselessly. He turned twice in the air, and the ground rose up to strike him in the face. He peered through a haze of blood and pain, and saw the newcomers walk forward with calm purpose. Two of his men exited the guard post with weapons in hand, looking around in confusion. Steerman tried to shout a warning, but the impostors had already raised compact alley-bows. Bolts thudded into his mens' flesh, and they toppled to the floor. The sergeant tried to rise, but his legs would not respond. Sigmar, it was hard to breathe. He was dimly aware of the smell of smoke. He looked down, and saw the ruin of his chest. Embers of blue fire danced across the tattered remains of his jacket.

He looked up, gasping for air. The blue-eyed traitor was standing in front of the storm engine, reading from the same scroll. Steerman couldn't hear the words, but he could hear the globe spit and hiss like a tormented beast. Fresh arcs of lightning surged across its surface, more violently than ever before. He coughed blood, and the impostor glanced across and met his eyes. Those cold blue eyes lit up with a smile, and the man gestured at Steerman with a finger. Another bolt of scorching blue flame screamed towards him, and the last thing he felt was the searing heat of it as it struck him in the face.

The Cult of the Fated Path seized control of their targets with ruthless efficiency. Unaware of the traitors in their midst, the garrison soldiers assigned to protect the arcane engines that powered Excelsis were taken by surprise and quickly disposed of. The words were spoken, as it had been ordained, and the proper rituals performed. One by one the great occulum fulgurest machines began to spit torrents of twisted magical energy into the heavens. The sky tore open. A purple bruise of tortured reality rippled and spread across the heavens. The sound was apocalyptic, a primal roar of creation and destruction. Screams began to echo through the streets as the inhabitants of Excelsis looked to the sky and saw what could only mean the end of their world.

A shockwave blasted out across the city, hurling people to the floor, ripping doors off hinges, smashing amberglass windows. Ships heaved and groaned in the harbour. Those closely moored clashed together violently, and the impact sent sailors stumbling and sliding across their decks, some tumbling helplessly into the churning waters. Far above the storm of rippling sails, the floating towers that surrounded the looming Spear of Mallus writhed with voltaic energy. Their twisted spires arced with forks of lighting, reaching out towards the Spear, sending chunks of displaced stone falling into the raging seas below. One tower was blasted out of its orbit, and smashed into the side of the great monolith. It carved a furrow through the Spear as it fell, before breaking in two. Both pieces fell into the harbour, splintering a trio of fat-bodied whaling cogs into kindling. Aetheric storms rippled across the surface of the Spear. The violence of their motion and the surging waters below gave the illusion that the monolith was rising clear of the waters to finally destroy the city that sat beneath it. But the real threat came from the rift above.

From the swirling void of tortured colours a great shape began to emerge. At first it was half-visible, as if some god-like being was dragging itself into the realm. As the tainted spheres continued to spit their poison into the sky, the image became clearer. A single crystal tower was visible, stabbing forth from the breach like the tip of a colossal spear. Behind this structure a greater fortress could be half-glimpsed through the chaos of the rift, a maddening cluster of turrets and spires that seemed in constant flux. Storm lightning arced around the emerging tower, flickering across its crystalline surface so brightly that it hurt the eye to observe. Dark clouds spewed forth from the rent in the world, racing towards the city below. No, not clouds. Swarms. Flocks of winged and writhing shapes shimmering in the pink light, eagerly anticipating the feast of souls and soft flesh that awaited them below. Great discs of irides-cent glass fell in their wake, and the glint of speartips and armour could be seen on top of them as they descended to cleave through the spires of ramshackle towers, crushing the frail city beneath them and spilling screeching warriors into the panicked streets.

'Throne of Sigmar,' whispered General Synor. The reflection of amberglass from the window of his office rendered the man's face a sickly yellow.

'There's your proof, general,' said Toll. 'There's the death of this city, unless you get your men out on the streets and ready to fight.'

The general stood there for a moment, mouth open and eyes wide with shock. Then, to Callis' surprise, he snapped into action. He leapt over the desk, scattering papers and spilling the decanter of wine, and swung the door to his office wide.

'Lieutenant Brellig, assemble the men,' he bellowed. 'I want them armed and eager in the courtyard this instant. Get our regiments out on the streets and ready to fight.'

The lieutenant's face was pale and his eyes wide, but he nod-ded and scurried off down the corridor. Already the halls of the bastion were filled with confused cries and the tramp of boots.

Synor turned to Toll, no hint of panic upon his face. His jaw was set, his gaze calm. *Some men only thrive in crisis*, Callis thought. 'Will you fight with us, Witch Hunter? I could use your advice.'

'You have it, general. We need to push forward to the Prophesier's Guild. I know what Kryn and Vermyre plan. It's just like your dream, Callis. The arcane engine above the Prophesier's Guild is the largest source of power in the city. That's where Kryn will be.'

The general nodded, and snapped his fingers at the guardsmen stationed outside his door. The soldiers formed up around the group, and together they hurried back to the courtyard, passing scores of milling soldiers and bellowing officers. They burst out of the great iron doors of the bastion, and gazed up at the bruised sky. Arcs of lightning flashed across the heavens, silhouetting bizarre discs that floated down from on high, and bat-like flocks of cackling monsters.

'What in Sigmar's name are you waiting for?' bellowed Synor at the gunners lining the walls, staring slack-jawed at the apocalypse falling from the sky. 'Start firing or I'll run you through myself.'

Dozens of cannons, mortars and ballistae swivelled into position on every battlement and watchtower, bracketing the creatures falling from the sky. Gunners sighted and adjusted, loaders crammed and wadded breeches, and then came the shouted warnings to cover ears and brace.

The Iron Bulls Bastion spat its defiance back at the abominations that dared to assault this blessed city of the God-King. The ground shook as several tonnes of shot and shrapnel were hurled forth. Many missed their target, but the skies were so thick with the enemy that even the first, target-finding strikes often struck home. Flocks of chortling, spiralling daemons were sent tumbling out of the sky, or simply shredded into a fine mist as spreadshot blasts tore through flesh and sinew. One of the great crystal discs arced over Callis' head, and he could see the spreading cracks in its translucent surface, rippling and bifurcating. With a scream of protest the transport came apart, raining glass and screaming bodies as it angled down to smash into the city wall, carving through stone and surrounding buildings, sending clouds of dust and shattered mortar into the air. A shard of falling crystal scythed through one of the volley-guns on the battlement to Callis' left, bisecting the crew, the cannon and the parapet with awful, surgical precision.

After a minute or so the first barrage ceased, and all that was left was a piercing ringing in Callis' ears, slowly fading. He could hear the sound of clattering boots and a chorus of confused, frightened voices as hundreds of guardsmen grabbed weapons and ammunition, threw on tunics and breastplates and hurtled down spiral stairways to the mustering yard.

'Form up! Form up!' Synor was hollering, as a pair of pale-faced adjutants buckled on the general's armour with trembling hands.

The great doors to the armoury swung open, and more green-clothed forms emerged, hauling the great weapons of war that were the pride of the city guard. Twin-racked volley guns, heavy duardin-forged cannons and the notoriously temperamental, yet undeniably effective, Ironweld rocket arrays. A low, angry rumble echoed out across the yard, audible even over the chaos of the skies above. From the armoury emerged another contraption, though this one needed no team of stocky, soot-covered engineers to haul it.

'The *Old Lady*,' said General Synor, with great affection. 'Let's see these traitors have a taste of her power.'

The steam tank rumbled forward on four heavy iron-bound wheels, belching smoke as it went. A hatch on top of the wedge-shaped contraption opened, and a bearded, goggled man emerged, skin cooked pink by the hellish heat of the interior cabin, face dusted with soot and grime. Mounted on the cupola of the steam tank was a long-barrelled rifle topped with a scope, and the man grasped the weapon and began to go through the process of cleaning and loading it.

By now most of the regiment's foot soldiers were lined up. Synor's greatsword-wielding honour guard stood at the fore, the biggest and strongest warriors in the company, their blades engraved with countless battle-honours and polished so brightly they shone even in the gathering gloom. Behind them stood the rank and file, armed with an array of blades, spears, shields and axes. Crossbowmen and handgunners checked muzzles and triggers, hefted their precious ammunition in leather quivers or goatskin pouches.

Callis felt a swell of pride at the sight, but there was no time to appreciate the swiftness with which Synor's men had pulled themselves together and made ready for war. Smoke rose in the distance, down near the harbour. The chorus of screams that echoed throughout the city was growing louder, and overhead the dark, swirling swarms were almost upon them. Shapes grew within the mass. Impossible forms, composed of twisted limbs and jabbering mouths.

'We must hurry,' said Toll. 'Vermyre's aiming to bring the rest of that citadel through the breach, and Sigmar help us all if he manages it.'

Synor was strapping on his scabbard, which carried a fine broadsword. His orderly came forward with the general's hat, a wide cap of deep green that bore three huge, white feathers and an emerald brooch fashioned in the shape of a falling comet.

With his accoutrements of war secured and fastened, and the hilt of his blade clasped in one gloved hand, even Callis had to admit that Synor looked every inch the dashing general. You couldn't even see the bulge of his gut. It was amazing what a dose of genuine crisis could do for some men.

'Well, gentlemen,' said General Synor, 'let us see to the defence of our city.'

ACT THREE

The men of the fighting Eighth roared across the stone cobbles, screaming their battle-oaths and prayers to Sigmar, brandishing swords, axes, maces and spears. These were hardened killers, men and women who had travelled the length of the Coast of Tusks, and battled almost every one of its myriad horrors. They would not be intimidated, even amidst the calamity that had fallen upon their city. Synor rode a chestnut warhorse at the head of the column, urging his men on with bellowed oaths of vengeance and promises of slaughter.

Streams of fleeing citizens filtered past them as they marched. There were hundreds of them. Thousands. Parents clutching bawling infants. Thin-limbed street urchins, eyes wide with fearful excitement. Many were limping, held up only by their fellows. Callis saw horrific burns, gashes and cuts from shattered glass. The pitiful figures flinched and cowered at every gunshot and explosion that echoed out across the city. In the distance, through the haze of fire-lit smoke, a formation of duardin gyrocopters arced over the city, the ear-aching, percussive thud of their rotating blades almost fading as they disappeared into the distance.

'The Air Corps will deal with as many of the enemy's flying monsters as they can,' shouted Synor above the commotion. 'But they are few. We cannot count on their presence.'

The cobbles flickered with the shadows of dancing flames, and the smoke was thick about them. Pitiful hands clawed at the soldiers as they passed. Bleeding, dust-covered figures staggered out of the smoke and fell to their knees in front of the advancing warriors, begging for salvation. There was no time to help them. No time to quell the fires that raged through the city, or to guide the innocent to safety.

Explosions echoed in the distance, along with the percussive blasts of heavy cannon and the shrieking whine of rockets arcing through the air. Above the cluttered rooftops the sky flashed orange, and smoke rose from the harbour. Apparently Captain Zenthe had made her choice. The Iron Bulls were not the only force that was fighting back.

'If we push through to the docks, we can join up with General Revard's Firewolves,' General Synor said.

'No,' said Toll, shaking his head. 'It will divert us from our target, and we cannot afford the delay.'

Synor stared at the conflagration in the distance, clearly torn.

'If we do not stop Kryn,' the Witch Hunter continued, 'it won't matter how many regiments we have fighting with us. The city will burn.'

The General nodded, grim-faced, and wheeled his horse around, urging his warriors forward.

Something sleek with iridescent scales flitted through the billowing blackness overhead, hissing and screeching. Something struggled beneath it, clutched in wicked talons. As the thing passed overhead, it released its burden. The half-naked man fell, screaming in terror, and was dashed to pieces on the cobbles. More shapes dropped out of the smoke. Callis saw myriad eyes mounted upon crescents of shimmering azure scales, rows of razor-sharp fangs and three-pronged tails that flitted gracefully behind as the shapes dived towards the column.

'Open fire!' shouted Synor. The handgunners did as they were bid, sending a hail of bullets skyward. Some of the creatures toppled out of the air. Most of them did not.

They scythed through the ranks of the Iron Bulls, a fountain of gore erupting in their wake. Callis fell to all fours as the wave passed overhead, and saw the man next to him yanked off his feet as if by a bolting horse.

'Reload and address! Reload and address, damn your eyes!' someone was bellowing. All around, soldiers were scrabbling to their feet, sliding on the blood-slick cobbles.

'No!' shouted Toll. 'We cannot stop here. Advance! Advance to the Grand Square.'

Synor glanced at the Witch Hunter. It was clear that he was unused to another issuing commands to his company, but thankfully the man seemed to have quelled whatever wounded pride he had displayed back in his office.

'You heard the man,' he bellowed. 'Keep moving! Do not stop for a moment.'

And so they hurried onwards, the ray-like monstrosities circling overhead like carrion birds, occasionally swooping down to spear another victim on those wicked fangs. Callis ran alongside the others, dimly aware of Toll at his side, retching and spluttering as the smoke seared his eyes and crept into his lungs. It was only the years of treading these streets that told him the wide thoroughfare they had stepped onto was the Tradeway, the arterial route that cut through the heart of Excelsis down to the harbour markets, passing the Grand Square and the Prophesier's Guild as it did so.

He ground his fist into his eyes and peered ahead, trying to get his bearings. In the distance he made out the great dome of the guildhall, rising above every other building in the square. The top of the structure had been shorn open. Lightning danced across the jagged edges of the opening and arced upwards into the sky, reaching with forked fingers towards the crystal tower emerging many thousands of feet overhead.

'Kryn's already at work,' growled Toll. 'We're running out of time.'

From the summit of the Prophesier's Guild, Ortam Vermyre could see the banners of the Iron Bulls coming ever closer. A regiment of middling reputation, as far as he could recall. Still, this was far from ideal.

'They regroup quickly,' he said. 'Far more quickly than we anticipated.'

He had hoped that the confusion and distrust his agents had sown throughout the city would prevent the Firewolves and the Iron Bulls from responding until his full force was on the field. The Coldguard, of course, were as good as his. The few known loyalists within their ranks would have been purged as soon as the regiment took to the field, as per his instructions. That purge would continue with the Firewolves, who would be surrounded and slaughtered by the Coldguard as soon as they set foot out of their bastion. They would not even know their doom until their own allies opened fire. But he was not pleased to see the Iron Bulls muster so quickly. He had hoped that General Synor's regiment would be bogged down in fighting through the streets. The Iron Bulls were a pious and obstinate bunch of zealots that he had never successfully infiltrated beyond a few eyes and ears in the ranks. The speed at which they had assembled about the guildhall was certainly an unpleasant surprise. That would not save them from the forces at his disposal, of course, but it was still a complication that he could have done without.

'Let them march,' came Kryn's death rattle of a voice, rife with a surge of excitement that to Vermyre's ears made him sound even more hideous than usual. The mage paced around the great occulum fulgurest, a heavy tome clutched in his claw-like hands. The machine was raised on a bronze-cast walkway suspended on mighty chains high above the auction hall that spread out beneath them, connected by a bewilderingly intricate array of binding pipework that led far above them to the ceiling, and trailed far below to the three great crystal jars in which the swirling mists of fate siphoned from the Spear of Mallus were contained. These containers loomed over the empty space of the great hall, secured behind a heavy fence of copper bars that reached some twenty feet into the air. In front of this were seven raised and heavily secured vendor booths, nothing less than blocky, armoured bunkers with viewing ports and a bolted access tube.

They took security seriously at the Prophesier's Guild. Or at least they had, until Vermyre had murdered those guild members loyal to the city, and replaced them with his own men.

The High Arbiter was distracted once more by Kryn's wheezing laughter. The old wretch was giddy at the prospect of unleashing his magic on the city, and earning the favour of his dark liege. Sparks and fleeting symbols danced from his fingers as he enacted another spell, binding the whirring occulum to his will. His servants, towering metal automatons of brass with faces carved in the likeness of hunting falcons, strode about the device and its crown of pipework, rearranging the machinery to the wizard's exact specifications. Kryn cajoled, insulted and bellowed at the golems as if they were clumsy-handed servants, and not mindless metal statues bound together by magic.

Vermyre watched him work. How different things were now. The arrogant wizard had once been a studiously loyal servant of Sigmar. The High Arbiter's initial attempts to plant the seeds of heresy in

Kryn's mind had been furiously, violently rebuffed. He had lost a whole cadre of trusted agents, burned to cinders in the fury of the wizard's rage. But Vermyre was not a man to give up easily. It had taken him several long, hard years of work. The right tomes, planted where Kryn would happen upon them. Some political manoeuvres, denying him the unrestricted access to the Spear of Mallus he so craved. Hundreds, thousands of other subtle machinations, all designed to massage the old wretch's pride and erode his loyalties. All had led to this moment. Yet everything might be for naught if the ancient, addled mage was not given the time to work his magics.

'Don't look so worried, Vermyre. You think a few thousand witless thugs can stop what is happening?' laughed Kryn. 'They will burn. Look above us! Our moment is here. The city will burn, and almighty Tzeentch will have his bounty.'

Vermyre glanced upwards at the tortured sky, visible through the circular, stained glass windows far above. The crystal tower inched ever closer into the realm, a knife hovering above the heart of the city. Already the servants of the Lord of Sorcery were pouring down upon Excelsis, eager to tear down this blasphemous illusion of order and control. Once the fortress in the sky had fully emerged, the armies at his disposal would be beyond count. Beyond even the ability of the errant Stormcast hosts to turn aside. The realm of Chaos would spill across the Coast of Tusks, and the process of siphoning the secrets and prophecies of the Spear of Mallus could begin. What could be more tempting to a god of fate than such a prize? The citizenry would be fed to the skyspawn builder-organisms, becoming raw matter, moulded into new towers, arches and spires. When the Stormcasts returned to Excelsis, they would find it a fortress of roiling transmutative magic. And as with all the others, they would burn in the fires of change.

Despite himself, despite the necessity of his work, Vermyre felt a tinge of sadness. This city had been good to him these many years. He would miss the power he had wielded here, the challenge of weaving his web of intrigue under the noses of the Order of Azyr and the bloodhounds of the Knights Excelsior.

'It is necessary,' he said to himself.

'Eh?' snapped Kryn, pausing from his work on the occulum to raise a quizzical eyebrow at Vermyre.

'Only great Tzeentch offers eternal change. Apotheosis,' Vermyre said, louder this time. 'These fools, they believe this dream can last. That it can stand in the face of true power. Eternal power. If only they recognised the truth of it.'

'They are insects,' spat Kryn. 'Vermin. Devouring prophecy like cheap wine, imagining they have any right to such power. When this city is no more, and the crystal tower stands in the sky above, the secrets of the Spear will finally be mine. By Tzeentch's will I shall know it all. My eyes will pierce the veil of fate, and I will know... the infinity of truth.'

Vermyre studied the old man, whose eyes had glazed over with rapturous desire. Arrogance and greed, that was all that kept this ancient skeleton together. He was a pathetic creature, really, for all his wizardly might. He could never appreciate the salvation that the God of Change offered, could not see beyond his petty lust for power. He would have to be removed, once he had served his purpose. Vermyre wondered whether his own master would agree. The former High Arbiter was a bold man, but he would not risk going against the will of Tzeentch.

Worries for another time. He turned back to look out over the city. The day was not yet won. The Cult of the Fated Path had revealed itself, playing its final hand. Now it must keep the loyalist forces on the back foot until it was too late.

'Finish your work quickly, Kryn,' he said, heading for the spiral stairway that would lead him down onto the main floor of the guildhall. 'I have an army to destroy.'

In the guildhall below, his own army waited. His trusted men, the Fatesworn, stood waiting for him at the foot of the great stairwell. They had abandoned their civilian masks. There was no call for secrecy any more. Now they wore elaborate pauldrons and vambraces of witch-forged metal, shendyts of blue and many-eyed battle-masks of gold. Their bare chests were littered with tattooed oaths of devotion in the tongue of their dread masters, and alongside their gleaming silver weapons they bore scrolls and tomes of profane lore. The ten warriors of his personal guard fell in behind Vermyre silently as he walked, scores more waiting in their ranks and files.

Altogether more unpredictable allies filled the rest of the hall. Tall and muscular creatures. Humanoid, yet avian in aspect, with clawed feet, beaks as sharp as daggers, and horns that swept back from their arrow-like skulls. They gazed at the cultists through blazing red eyes that shone like glowing embers, without fear, but with a detached, alien interest. They bore armour and weapons even finer than their human allies, doubtless spell-forged within the sacred labyrinth-halls of the crystal fortresses. They smelled of brimstone and sorcerous ritual. Tzaangors. The elusive, secretive footsoldiers of mighty Tzeentch.

Their leader drifted forwards on a disc of living metal that pulsed with hungry energy. Despite himself, Vermyre could not help but be impressed by the imposing figure. This Tzaangor bore a staff of obsidian tipped with a swirling, sickly green vortex. The eye of Tzeentch was emblazoned upon the belt of jewels and gold around its waist, and above a ceremonial helm two horns curled backwards like those of a ram.

'We came to slay,' it hissed, in a voice that sounded like a knife scraping across stone, 'not to wait. Not to hide. We go forth. We gather human-meat for the sky-engines. For the glory of the Lord of Eyes.'

Vermyre nodded. He had rarely dealt with these strange, tribal creatures, and he did not imagine for a moment that they would take orders from a human. As befitting for the God of Change, a leadership role within the ranks of the Kairic Cults was by necessity an amorphous thing.

'They are coming here,' he said, meeting the shaman's cruel eyes and not blinking for a moment. 'You will defend the square. Their attack will be scattered and weak. Rout them, but capture as many as you can. The crystal tower must be fed with new fuel.'

Sykarik threw his head back and screeched, a shrill, ululating sound. It was answered as one by the Tzaangor warriors that lined the guildhall.

Finally the Iron Bulls broke out of the smoke clouds, and the great open space of the plaza opened up before them, a field of finely worked greystone slabs dotted with trees and statuary. On all sides of the open forum, basilicas, halls and galleries rose, their columns engraved with further images of Sigmar's glory, statues of mighty warriors and pious saints raised beneath the shadow of their soaring arches. On any normal day, this beating heart of commerce would have been thronged by merchants, bureaucrats and politicians, as well as those looking to bid on the latest and most promising auguries freshly mined from the Spear.

On this day, it was occupied by the host of the invading horde.

There were thousands of them arrayed in loose formation before the guildhall. Mutated forms, vaguely humanoid yet utterly alien, they were taller by a head than the average man and their bodies were lithe and predatory, their narrow heads avian in aspect and topped by curved horns capped with bronze and silver. They bore wondrous silver weapons and armour – curved blades, vicious war-picks and hooked longspears – and their war-masks, torcs and hooped piercings shone gold and turquoise. Banners flew above their numbers, depicting writhing serpents, two-headed crows and unblinking, glowing eyes. As the Iron Bulls rushed to form up at the other end of the plaza, the bestial figures began to shriek and caw in high-pitched, unnervingly musical tones. The sonorous boom of a war-horn echoed across the empty ground between the two forces.

It was answered by the battle-drums of the Iron Bulls.

'Form ranks,' shouted the sergeants, jostling and hauling their men into position. The great guns clattered and groaned as they were hauled forward, set up in the mouths of the southern buildings, with a slight elevation of range.

'They wait for us,' said Toll, eyeing the strange avian beastmen. 'They're guarding the guildhall.'

'Not for long,' growled Synor. He hauled his warhorse about, facing his warriors, and raised his broadsword into the air. The horse reared and snorted.

'Men of the Eighth!' he roared, and his voice carried even above the abominable clatter that the *Old Lady* made as it rolled into position at the head of the line. 'We have been betrayed. Heretics, worshippers of the Dark Gods and heathen monsters plan to destroy this city. Our city! Before you stand their twisted servants, and beyond them lies the great hall of the Prophesier's Guild. This is where the arch-traitors Ortam Vermyre and Velorius Kryn cower, believing that the day is already won.'

He fixed the soldiers of the Iron Bulls with a steel gaze, and trotted his horse down the line with his blade raised in salute.

'Is that so, warriors of the Iron Bulls of Tarsus?' he shouted. 'Are you defeated yet?'

'NO!'

The screams and war cries of the Eighth answered proudly. Even Callis found himself bellowing along with the rest.

Synor wheeled about, and aimed his sword straight at the heart of the enemy formation.

'Forward, warriors of the Eighth!'

The fighting Eighth were an old and storied regiment, tested on the field of battle all across the Coast of Tusks. When the first colonists had arrived in Excelsis, the Iron Bulls had been there to spill their own blood in the name of peace and order, buying a future for their children with their lives. That noble tradition continued on the bloody steps of the Prophesier's Guild. The front ranks of the Eighth met the enemy with shields raised and songs of praise to their warrior-god upon their lips. The enemy howled and counter-charged, bounding over the marble of the grand square with unnatural grace, their powerful, backwards-jointed limbs giving them the rangy stride of a predatory bird. They hurled themselves into the fray with shrieks of battle-joy, silver swords flickering in the gloom. Other beastmen rose above the battle on discs of warped metal and strange organic material, wielding greatbows as tall as a mortal man. From these impressive weapons they unleashed a storm of sparkling arrows that flickered blue-green as they fell upon the Iron Bulls formation. The creatures seemed to be shooting randomly, but Toll knew better.

'Protect the gun crews,' he urged General Synor. 'These creatures, they will aim for vital targets – officers, gunners, standard bearers. They look to disrupt our attack.'

Synor shouted orders, and several squads of swordsmen dropped back to provide cover for the artillery, enveloping the gun crews and raising their shields. Many of the flickering arrows sparked and spat as they deflected off the wall of steel, but the creatures were exceptional shots. Several gunners collapsed, twitching, pierced by the shimmering missiles. To Toll's left, a lieutenant barking orders to his men abruptly sighed and slumped to the floor, an arrow protruding from the back of his neck.

In the midst of the flying archers another figure rose, wrapped in robes of vibrant turquoise, horns swept back like those of a ram, face concealed behind a jade mask with eyes that burned like hot coals. This creature carried a staff of obsidian, topped with a baleful eye of green. It swept its weapon low, and a gout of blue-white fire spat from the eye of the staff, setting a dozen mortals alight. Their screams echoed over the clangour of battle.

'They will hold,' muttered Synor, viewing the carnage from the rear of the Iron Bulls' line.

Callis felt a fierce pride as he watched these brave men and women defend their home, not giving an inch despite the horrors that had been unleashed upon them. Grim-faced halberdiers held the line against the fury of the beastmen, spitting defiance at their foe even as eldritch arrows screamed into their ranks, turning flesh to smoke and crystal, burning soldiers away as if they had never existed. Against the power and sorcery of the beastmen, the formations of soldiers were almost laughably outmatched. No matter. They held their ground, shields raised, and for every loyal Sigmarite that fell to the wicked curved swords of the foe, another rushed forwards to take their place.

It could not last. More of the ray-like flying predators shrieked through the air, carving into the Iron Bulls' battle line, snatching up screaming figures and releasing them to be dashed to pieces on the marble below. From the darkness of the basilicas on each side of the plaza came a tide of masked warriors, chests bare and scrawled with unholy symbols and forbidden text, faces concealed behind leering masks of gold and silver. Some loosed bolts of flesh-melting green energy from wands and sceptres, while others cleaved into the flanks of the Iron Bulls with daggers and axes. The human face of the invasion had revealed itself at last.

The general urged more of his men forward, sending his reserve into the thick of the melee to clear the cultists. Crossbowmen and handgunners bracketed the ambushers with raking volleys, sending scores tumbling to the floor with smoking holes bored in their exposed flesh, quarrels protruding from their necks. The smell of cordite was strong enough to make Callis gag.

'We're containing them,' said Synor, observing the battle from the steps of an abandoned counting hall at the southern edge of the square. 'But that won't last. We have no support, and those damned flying creatures are slaughtering us.'

'Sir!' came a cry from their right. 'The artillery is in position. But the battle lines are drawn so close we risk hitting our own men.'

'Fire!' snapped Synor. 'Trust in your gun crews, captain. Without ordnance this battle is lost regardless, and we're all dead.'

The general turned to Toll. 'We'll give them a barrage, and then I'll give the order to push forward. It'll be a bloody affair, Witch Hunter.'

'If Kryn corrupts the occulum arrays and brings that abomination into our skies, the city entire will burn,' said Toll. 'You're making the right choice, general. Our only hope lies in spending our deaths wisely.'

Callis heard the shouts from down the line, and covered his ears instinctively. The cannons were spaced out amongst the columns of the structure to their right, the abandoned remnants of what was normally the Hall of Justice. Now it bristled with all manner of Ironweld field pieces – great, wide-barrelled siege cannons, four-chambered organ guns, black and yellow marked rocket arrays. The gunmasters were there, peering through their sight-glasses, roaring last minute orders to the gun crews.

Then the world shook with fire. A billowing cloud of sour smoke erupted from the mouth of the Hall of Justice, and several score balls of solid metal were vomited forth at the ranks of the enemy.

Beastmen and cultists simply disappeared, their flesh blasted apart so fast that they seemed to simply transform into clouds of crimson mist. The cannonballs continued on, arcing and bouncing through the massed ranks, leaving immeasurable carnage in their wake. The accuracy of the fire was impressive, a hallmark of the Iron Bulls' skilful gun crews, yet not every shot struck true. Callis' heart sank to see his fellow soldiers torn asunder by inevitable misplaced shots.

'Their deaths are no less noble,' growled Synor, noticing the guardsman's unease. 'The mathematics of war is rarely palatable.'

He drew his broadsword, three and a half feet of gleaming steel, with a bucket hilt forged in the shape of a rearing bull.

'Let's get this underway, then,' he said. 'Witch Hunter, shall I assume you'll join me in the charge?'

Toll was already checking the lock of his four-barrelled pistol. Callis did the same with Kazrug's duardin-forged piece, and adjusted his uncle's sword at his side.

'After you, general,' said the Witch Hunter.

The *Old Lady* led the way. The steam tank spat streams of smoke as it rumbled towards the right flank of the enemy, shaking the earth beneath its great iron-shod wheels. With a thunderous roar, the tank's main gun fired. The cannonball was almost too fast to see, but the mist of gore and the flying chunks of meat it left in its wake were impossible to miss. The *Old Lady* barely slowed at all. The gunner atop the iron monstrosity blasted away with the axle-mounted rifle, stopping occasionally to bellow orders down into the cabin below.

Toll, Synor and Callis followed in its wake, accompanied by the general's elite bodyguard in their gleaming, golden armour. Cultists, dazed and confused by the brutality of the assault, stumbled out of the great smoke trail the tank left behind it. The greatswords of the general's guard hacked them apart, easily cleaving through the scant armour that the masked mortals wore. Callis saw a tall, thin cultist on the steps of a building to their right, one arm outstretched as he chanted foul phrases in some alien tongue, aiming a glowing crystal sceptre towards the *Old Lady*. He raised Kaz-rug's gun and put a bullet through the man's gut, blasting him off his feet and sending him rolling down the stairs, howling in pain. The man came to a rest in a crumpled heap, his mask slipping free to reveal a round, boyish face and white-blonde hair. Callis' gut tightened. He recognised the man, a guardsman named Erigard. He had lost to him at cards only a few weeks past.

Arrows and spells were hissing and fizzling as they struck the steam tank's hull. The iron was thick, and it would not yield, but the *Old Lady* was beginning to rock and squeal with protest under the barrage. Cultists leapt upon the frame of the vehicle, dragging themselves towards the top hatch. The gunner dropped the axle-mounted rifle and drew a wide-bore pistol. The first masked face to haul itself over the lip of the side armour exploded in a welter of brain matter. Another figure was clubbed to the floor, and yet more fell to missiles hurled by their own side.

'Clear the way!' shouted Synor, gesturing at the ranks of cultists that were pouring fire into the *Old Lady* from between a row of marble columns to their right. 'Bring those spellcasters down, now!'

But they could not reach them. The steam tank continued to fire its main cannon, reaping a horrible toll on the enemy ranks before it, but even the thick iron armour that protected its flanks was beginning to come apart.

There was a shrill hissing sound, and cutting through the air came the flying disc of the beastman sorcerer who had unleashed its fire upon the sword infantry. The creature ignored the crossbow bolts that clattered off the daemonic device that bore it aloft, and raised its sickly-green staff again. A fist of magical flame rushed out to slam the *Old Lady* in the flank. The gunner toppled out of his hatch, striking the cobbled ground hard. The tank groaned in protest, and began to rear on its side, the power of the magical flame melting thick bands of metal and superheating the vehicle.

Callis could hear the screams of the driver team as they began to roast alive. He brought his pistol to bear and it bucked in his hand, but though his and Toll's shots were true, they had no effect upon the avian sorcerer.

The heat cooked off the *Old Lady*'s powder reserve. The resulting fireball lifted the twelve-ton tank into the air, where it spun once before crashing to the marble floor and rolling. It crushed the poor gunner beneath its awful weight, as well as dozens of cultists too slow to hurl themselves out of the way.

The shockwave blasted Callis, Toll and the front ranks of the general's men clean off their feet. They slammed down hard, groaning and choking as a fresh cloud of smoke billowed over them. Callis struggled to his knees. Synor lay a few paces ahead, trying to free his legs from beneath his horse, which lay unmoving. He had no idea where the Witch Hunter was. Through the cloud of smoke, masked faces began to appear. Callis aimed and fired at one, and the man dropped, clutching at a gaping hole in his throat. More emerged, scores of them, wielding long, curved daggers.

'Get up!' he screamed, as the soldiers around him lurched groggily. He fumbled at his belt, found the hilt of his uncle's sabre and drew it. 'They're coming! Reform the line!'

It was too late. The enemy was only a few paces away now, and their daggers gleamed in the light of the fires. They leapt upon the staggered Iron Bulls, hacking and stabbing, bearing down the more heavily armoured soldiers with sheer weight of numbers. Callis swayed aside as a masked figure lurched at him, sliced the man's leg off below the knee with a wild swing of his sabre. Smoke billowed all around. He could not see further than a half-dozen yards in any direction. Shapes swirled around him.

Something colossal strode through the smoke. It was twice the size of a man, and many times as broad, with a rolling, bestial gait that hinted at appalling strength. Two ridged horns swept back from its monstrous head, and it clutched a staff topped with the skull of a beast in its oddly dextrous hands. Sickly green-blue smoke poured from its eye sockets. A muscular tail whipped around the creature's hooved legs.

It stopped, and scanned the devastation before it.

Its eyes locked with Callis'. The beast smiled.

Callis was up before the thought of running even entered his head, staggering away into the smoke cloud, weaving his way through broken bodies and the wreckage of the steam tank. The ground shook beneath him, the steady pace of the nightmare creature as it paced after him. He could barely hear a thing over the ringing in his ears.

Something struck him hard in the back, and suddenly he was sailing through the air. He might have been screaming, but it was too hard to tell.

He turned over in the air before landing hard on something at once soft and full of hard edges. He glanced down, and saw a pile of corpses, a roughly half-and-half blend of green-jacketed Iron Bulls and lean, tattooed cultists. He put a hand down to prop himself up, and it sank up to the elbow in something warm and sticky. The ground shook again. He turned. The horned beast strode after him. Three Iron Bull swordsmen staggered into view, holding each other up, bleeding from a dozen wounds. The creature lazily waved its staff at them, and from the blazing sockets of the skull a tongue of azure flame spat forth. It wrapped around the Iron Bulls, and they screamed and thrashed silently before toppling to the floor, smouldering.

The beast kept on coming at Callis, still leering through its maw of jagged fangs. Callis stumbled on all fours, and staggered away into a row of columns that loomed out of the mist ahead of him. The ringing in his ears was fading now, and he could hear the faint drumbeat of cannon fire and shrill screams drifting above the chaos of battle. He staggered and fell, turned and scampered backwards on his hands as the creature approached. It stood before him, raised its staff and pointed the blazing skull directly at his face. He could smell scorched metal and strange, bitter spices.

More shapes filtered through the mist. Their torsos were inked and scarred, and they wore masks of horrifying aspect. They carried long curved daggers, and a variety of other weapons. Hateful, sickening symbols of devotion were emblazoned on deep blue robes or scorched upon bare flesh. They were chanting, a low droning sound in a language that turned Callis' stomach and sent a dull agony rippling through his skull.

The creature leaned down; Callis smelt its sulphurous breath, and looked deep into eyes that swirled with a hateful intelligence that seemed so incongruous with such a bestial form.

'Il'a konac v'y'oren,' it murmured. *'Hiem vo konac il'yor.'*

Lightning flashed, so bright that Callis gasped and raised a hand to cover his aching eyes. He heard a crash, almost as loud as the explosion that had destroyed the *Old Lady*, and a guttural bellow.

Giants strode amongst the enemy, crushing and hewing them with weapons as tall as a mortal human. They wore white, glistening white, and emanated a radiant brightness that seemed to cut straight through the overcast gloom and the drifting smoke.

'Throne of Sigmar,' whispered Callis reverentially. It was the first time he had ever seen the Stormcast Eternals in battle. He knew he would never forget the sight.

The enemy was not even falling back. The shock and the speed with which the giants slew did not give them the chance. They raised their daggers and sceptres high in an almost laughable attempt to defend themselves. The white giants simply swept them aside with arcing blows from silver warhammers and gleaming broadswords. The torn chunks of meat that had once been the traitor formation littered the ground. Broken bodies sailed through the air. Armoured feet stamped down on mewling creatures, crushing necks and skulls. There was no rage in the giants' actions, only pitiless and functional brutality.

The horned creature was bellowing in outrage, matching blows with three of the gleaming warriors. It hammered one aside with a mighty swing of its staff, and as the fallen Stormcast crashed against a pillar, sending chunks of chiselled stonework flying through the air, the creature called forth another blast of eldritch flame to engulf him. The fallen warrior rolled and writhed, his fine armour dancing with blue fire. His fellows spared no concern for their fallen brother, closing the gap on the giant and striking from two sides with their broadswords. The beast slammed one warrior to the ground with its staff, roaring as the other sank his blade into its ribs. It rammed its massive skull into the offending Stormcast's chest, sending him reeling backwards, and raised its staff to cast another spell.

A figure crashed into the beast's flank, striking so fast it seemed little more than a blur. Despite its huge size, the horned beast was thrown to the ground. This time its roar ended in a wet, choking gurgle. A sword flashed out, tearing through the beast's muscular neck with contemptuous ease. The hideous maned head rolled free, and a figure loomed above the broken corpse.

Callis felt his blood run cold. The White Reaper stood before him, his pristine armour marred with crimson. The blank eyes of his war-mask bored through Callis.

'Get up,' said the Reaper.

He got up.

'You saw Kryn in your vision,' said the Lord-Veritant. 'Lead me to him.'

Toll and a few surviving members of Synor's elite hauled away the general's fallen horse, freeing the officer's legs.

The general grunted in pain as his men pulled him to his feet.

His white dress trousers were stained crimson at the knee. Toll suspected the man had suffered a serious wound, but Synor stared down anyone who attempted to inspect his injuries.

'Enough,' he barked. 'We have no time for this. We must push through to the guildhall.'

'Our forces are scattered,' said a lieutenant with a nasty burn on the side of his face. A soldier was wrapping the wound with a makeshift bandage torn from his own tunic. 'We have no answer to their sorcery. The guns are quiet.'

It was true. The concussive blasts of the cannon and rocket arrays had ceased. Either the crews had been killed, or they could not pick out targets through the thick smoke that billowed across the battlefield.

'You heard the general,' Toll bellowed. 'Forward, make safe the guildhall!'

He knew it was futile. Already the avian beastmen and masked cultists were upon them, charging out of the smoke to hurl themselves at the ragged company. Screams and the clashing of blades rent the air. There were so many of them. An arrow whipped in and struck the burn-marked lieutenant in the chest, and he sagged into his soldier's arms with a heavy sigh. The enemy was attacking from all angles, and the hundred or so Iron Bulls that Toll could see were pushed tighter and closer together, desperately fending off the hordes of screeching beastmen with spears and handgun stocks. There was no way out. Toll drew his pistol, scanning the crowd for a sign of Callis. Nothing. He hoped by some miracle the lad had gotten away, but in his gut he knew better.

'Make them pay,' he shouted. 'Make them pay for every fallen comrade. Sigmar is watching, men and women of Excelsis. Let us scour these foul creatures from the face of our great city!'

All around him the warriors of the Iron Bulls roared their defiance and prepared to meet their end.

Their cries were met by the sound of chanting. A deep, sonorous song, a battle dirge that chilled the blood. Toll knew what it was, and the fading hope in his chest was kindled anew.

The Stormcasts had come. They hit the right flank of the beastmen and cultists like a battering ram, a wall of shields and stabbing swords that swept over the enemy like a rogue wave. There were not many of them, perhaps a few-score against hundreds of the foe. That was enough. Shields slammed out, shattering ribcages and crushing skulls. Blades followed in simple, disciplined thrusts. It was almost like watching some mechanical war machine of the Ironweld. They did not slow, nor did they cease their chanting. It rose above the clangour like the promise of death, and the masked cultists wavered in terror.

'Into them!' shouted Synor, brandishing his blade. 'Strike now!'

The combined charge of two-score Knights Excelsior and the remnants of the Iron Bulls pushed the invaders back to the steps of the Prophesier's Guild. The beastmen fought with a vicious fury, their sorcerous arrows and keen-edged blades reaping a horrible toll upon the defenders of Excelsis. Yet even they could not stand before the implacable might of the warriors in white. The Stormcasts battled at the tip of the spear, launching themselves into the ranks of the foe, battering and smashing the avian creatures aside with their Heavens-forged sigmarite weaponry. No warrior of Sigmar could fail to be inspired by the sight, even if it was the dreaded Knights Excelsior that carried the charge.

The avian beastmen fell back into the guildhall, the great arcane machinery spitting and protesting overhead as the battle raged. Those cultists that could follow suit did so, while the rest were hacked apart beneath the vengeful blades of the Iron Bulls. The regiment charged through the great iron doors of the Prophesier's Guild, Synor's personal guard at their head. The great hall soared high overhead, the domed ceiling barely visible beyond the hanging walkway that housed the occulum fulgurest. Toll could see figures up there, tiny and pale. The arcane machine spat filthy energy into the sky through a great rent torn in the domed ceiling, bathing the hall in a sickly pink light. The air warped in the far corners of the chamber, became greasy and oil-slick. Wretched, gibbering forms tumbled through these rents in space, giggling and skipping as they bounded towards the soldiers of the Eighth. They were little more than fleshy maws housed in torsos of violent pink, surrounded by a shifting, warping array of gangly limbs. As they leapt across the hall, they conjured streams of eldritch flame that seared through shields and devoured flesh.

One of the things bounded up to Toll, clapping its hands together like an eager child and chortling manically. It leapt at him, teeth gnashing for his face. He angled his blade and leaned to the side, letting the thing impale itself upon the blade. It gurgled and choked on foul purple ichor, still chortling idiotically. Then it collapsed into two separate chunks of torn meat. The clay-like flesh twisted and reformed, darkening and roiling with chaotic energy. New limbs emerged, and two new and identical faces took shape, leering daemonic visages that snapped and hissed at each other. The Witch Hunter levelled his pistol and blasted one of the blue monsters to pieces. Each fragment of the creature's flesh took on yet another form, this time several tiny, dancing flames that scattered underfoot, hissing furiously and snapping at ankles. The remaining blue horror scampered away, its limbs flailing and rancid spittle drooling from its chortling mouth.

Toll scanned the battlefield. His eyes locked on a small, unremarkable and yet recognisable figure duelling an Iron Bull swordsman, backed by a cadre of blood-smeared cultists. Toll watched the former High Arbiter Ortam Vermyre step aside to avoid a clumsy sword stroke before plunging his rapier into the unfortunate soldier's chest. Vermyre kicked the corpse free, and looked up to meet Toll's eyes.

'You are mine,' muttered the Witch Hunter, striding towards the traitor.

Armand Callis hurtled up the last few steps and burst out onto the walkway that hung suspended over the carnage of the guild-hall below. Arcane machinery pulsed and thrummed on all sides, and the metal path beneath his feet shook and groaned in protest. With a startling roar, a spear of lightning shot from the great sphere that loomed over their heads. It arced into the air, tearing through the roof above them and sending chunks of masonry and shards of broken amberglass raining all around. Looking up, Callis felt the sickness of vertigo. The sky above was an open wound, a seething maelstrom of black storm clouds and baleful, bruised-purple light. He could see the crystal tower that had stabbed its way into this realm, and behind it, looming like something half-glimpsed beneath the surface of a roiling sea, was the greater fortress. Though still obscured by the warped clouds, it was becoming clearer and more distinct with every passing moment.

He and the Lord-Veritant's soldiers clattered along the walkway. It curved around the bulk of the whirling occulum sphere, and opened into a large, semi-circular platform dominated by a collection of levers, gears and unknowably complex mechanisms that rippled with fingers of sapphire energy.

Before this strange device stood Velorius Kryn.

The old archmage clutched a tome bound in pale leather in a claw-like hand. He was muttering arcane phrases that made Callis' head thrum painfully. Beneath him, burned into the brass of the platform, was a dizzying array of symbols, arranged in perfect order like a mathematical equation.

Sentanus had with him six warriors. Three held greatswords, one a wicked-looking longaxe, another a device that looked more like a portable ballista than anything, and the final warrior bore two shorter blades that were still almost as large as Callis. They spread out in a semi-circle behind the Lord-Veritant, whose gaze was locked on the wizard Kryn.

'Heretic,' the White Reaper growled. 'Turn and face your death.'

Kryn seemed to only now notice the group. He turned, and Callis felt a cold shiver as he gazed into those eyes he knew so well for the first time. They shone with mad ambition, and Kryn's thin, pale lips creased into a wide grin. He seemed even more wizened and drawn than he had appeared in Callis' dream. His skin was maggot-white, stretched so thin over his bones that he looked more like a risen corpse than a living man.

'Welcome,' he cackled. 'You are just in time, Lord-Veritant. Or should I call you the Reaper? Simple-minded men like you do so love their sobriquets, do they not?'

Sentanus did not even seem to move, but suddenly his staff was lowered and a spear of blinding light burst from the lantern mounted at its tip. It struck Kryn in the chest, and his frail form was hurled across the platform, his own staff and tome tumbling away. The old wretch rolled to a halt, and Callis could hear his pained wheezing.

'You are done, wizard,' said Sentanus, the lantern light of his staff fading.

There was a choked, rattling sound. Callis realised that it was Kryn. He was laughing. The wizard staggered to his feet, and his hands formed grasping claws. He slowly lifted off the brass platform, shimmering particles of metal condensing underneath his feet in magnetic circles. His black iron staff whipped through the air into his waiting clutch, and Kryn span it in his hands, muttering an arcane phrase as he did so.

A few yards from the Stormcasts, the brass floor of the platform folded and rose into the air, like an inverted raindrop. It rippled and split apart, forming three roughly humanoid shapes that towered over Sentanus and his men. Their torsos and faces were as smooth and featureless as a dressmaker's mannequin, but their forelimbs ended in wicked hooks. The brass golems advanced upon the Stormcasts, weapon-limbs raised.

Sentanus roared in fury and leapt forward, drawing his great blade. His fellows charged in his wake, bellowing their battle oaths. Callis threw himself to the side as the monsters clashed together.

There was a resignation and, Toll fancied, a hint of sadness in Vermyre's eyes as he turned to face the Witch Hunter. The raging battle around them seemed to fade into the distance. Vermyre readied his blade, a simple rapier of silvered steel, unadorned but clearly well made. His cadre of cultists stepped forward, brandishing their own long knives, but Vermyre barked an order at them and reluctantly they slipped away, leaving the two former friends alone in the midst of the chaos that was tearing through the guildhall.

'Is it not fate, Hanniver?' the former High Arbiter said, and shook his head with a smile. 'That we would meet here, I mean. I was a fool to believe my dungeon could hold you.'

'I am going to kill you, Ortam.'

Vermyre shook his head. 'You forget, old friend, this is not the first time we have sparred. You're a fair enough duellist, Witch Hunter, but you've never comprehended the art of it.'

'That was practise. This is real.'

With that the Witch Hunter came forward, leading with an eye-level thrust. Vermyre stepped back, not even raising his own blade. Toll whipped his rapier out and jabbed forward twice more, seeking to score a lethal wound and end this fight quickly.

Vermyre swayed left then spun on one foot, pirouetting to the right and flipping his blade to his off hand as he did so. He let the turn add momentum to a low slice, and Toll felt a searing pain across his thigh.

'Ah, it's been too long since we last danced,' the traitor said, twirling the rapier in a mocking salute. 'You're getting old, Hanniver. A novice could have seen that coming. Too much time in the company of dull duardin, perhaps?'

Toll circled, testing his torn leg. A bad cut, but not a deep one. Foolish. Had Vermyre been wielding a longsword, the heavier blade would have likely taken his leg off.

He redressed and came forward again, high, high and low, a textbook attack routine. Vermyre swatted one thrust away before dancing out of the way of the second and third. Then he came forward in a rush, feinting at the gut and slicing across at head height. Toll barely got out of the way in time, feeling the rush of air as the rapier whipped past, catching the brim of his hat and tearing it from his head.

'Age betrays us all in the end,' said Vermyre, grinning at the Witch Hunter as if they were in on the same joke. 'If we allow it.'

Another flurry of strikes, exchanged so fast that Toll was reacting on pure instinct. Somehow he fended off the attack, giving ground and stumbling over the bodies that littered the floor. Vermyre came after him, now in a classic fencer's stance, one hand behind his back and his body angled to the side ready to slip out of the way of the Witch Hunter's ripostes.

The wizard's metal automatons were smashed apart and reformed, spinning back into the fray with a whir of twisting components. Sentanus held his staff high, and Callis could hear the low rumble as he chanted prayers of protection and binding. One of the Stormcasts went down, skewered by a pair of the brass golems, and as he toppled from the walkway, spinning end over end, his body disappeared in a blinding flash of lightning that rippled up through the broken ceiling. Kryn cackled with delight, still weaving spell after spell and hurling rays of searing fire and spheres of reality-warping power at the Knights Excelsior.

The crossbow-wielding Stormcast poured a torrent of radiant bolts into the surface of the metal creations, blasting away chunks of molten brass. One of the golems staggered under the barrage, and the warrior wielding a longaxe slammed his weapon into its chest, bringing it to the floor. The crossbow-wielder switched targets and began to blast away at the floating wizard. Kryn snarled in outrage as the volley sparked off the arcane shield that enveloped him, and pointed one wizened finger at the metal walkway beneath the shooter. The unfortunate Knight Excelsior was sucked into the brass that now grasped at his legs like quicksand. He disappeared into the metal, which reformed as if freshly wrought.

'You dare to threaten me?' shrieked Kryn. 'The arrogance of it. I will melt you inside those extravagant suits of armour.'

The air seemed to heat around the entire guildhall as he worked another spell. Thick chains of brass burst forth from the floor below, and with a gesture he sent them hurtling across the walkway. They struck the Stormcast with the duelling blades, lifting him from the floor and wrapping around him like the coils of a great snake. Callis could hear the awful sound of creaking metal. The chains looped around the unfortunate warrior's neck, and wrenched it backwards with a sickening crack that left the Stormcast limp. Another flash of lightning crackled up into the night. Kryn laughed until he coughed and hacked bloody spittle.

The White Reaper bellowed in fury. He smashed at the brass golem that was sprawled on the floor, hacking away at its featureless face with his blade. The Stormcast with the longaxe took aim at its bladed arms, trying to cut the limbs free. Sentanus lowered his staff, unleashed another beam of radiant energy, and the golem's head bubbled and dissolved. Its body followed suit, melting into the platform as if it had never existed. The remaining two warriors armed with greatswords faced the pair of brass golems that were still standing, avoiding the constructs' wild swings with surprising grace. One skipped past the heavy step of a golem, preparing a mighty swing that would strike the back of its leg.

Kryn screamed the words of another spell; a cloud of black iron daggers flittered through the air to sink into the attacking warrior's armour like a hail of arrows. He groaned and dropped to his knees, pulling at a blade that had sunk deep into his eye. His fellow Stormcast was now faced by two of the monstrosities. He blocked one swing and dodged another before a heavy brass foot slammed into his chest. He soared into the air, end over end, and crashed into the hanging machinery. His body slid to the floor, lightning already flickering around the ruin of his breastplate.

Sentanus and the warrior armed with the longaxe crashed into one of the remaining brass golems, hacking and slashing at its legs in an effort to bring it to the ground.

The other construct turned its eyeless gaze upon the only remaining threat.

'Oh, of course,' said Callis, and turned to run.

Toll stumbled, his boot sliding on a slick patch of blood. Vermyre was darting forward in an instant, a viper-quick thrust for his opponent's exposed neck. Toll got the rapier up just in time. Vermyre's blade slid along his own with a squeal of polished metal, and the two weapons locked at the hilt. Toll stared into the traitor's eyes, and saw nothing of the hate and madness that he expected. They were calm, dispassionate, as if the man was signing paperwork rather than duelling to the death with a friend he had known for decades.

'You're too slow, Hanniver,' said Vermyre. 'You can't win this fight. The power of the Changer of the Ways runs in my veins. I am his agent, and I will bring the light of change upon the free peoples of the realms.'

'You are a traitor and a murderer,' spat Toll, 'and when the time comes your soul will burn along with your foul master.'

He snapped his head forwards and felt Vermyre's nose crunch and erupt in a fountain of blood under the force of the blow. The former High Arbiter staggered back with a grunt of pain, and Hanniver slashed at his exposed throat.

Vermyre tried to fall backwards out of the way of the strike but it lashed across his face, blood spurting out. He clutched his hand to a ruined eye and howled. Hanniver saw his chance, and came forward with his rapier leading.

A moment before the Witch Hunter struck, Vermyre dropped his own blade and brought up his free hand, clutching a jewel-encrusted rod of silver, its tip aimed towards his assailant. There was an explosion of blue fire, and Toll felt himself soar through the air, flames licking at his flesh. He crashed to earth, groaning in agony, and rolled over to put out the blaze. His sword arm was a blistered mess of scorched red flesh, and the skin around his neck and shoulder thrummed with agony.

'When all else fails, fight dirty,' hissed Vermyre, coming forwards with the sceptre raised. 'I had forgotten who you truly were, Hanniver. A simple case of underestimation, and a plan long years in the making almost comes crashing down.'

Toll reached for a longsword that lay in the hands of a dead Iron Bull at his side, but Vermyre aimed the sceptre and another sheet of flame swept out to melt the weapon to slag.

'The truth is I wanted you at my side. I wanted you to understand why Sigmar's world must fall, and we must embrace a more challenging destiny. You could have done great things, Hanniver. I will mourn your loss. But I see now there is no opening your eyes. So be it.'

He raised the sceptre. It began to glow with a sickly blue light, and the former High Arbiter lowered it at Toll's chest.

'Goodbye, old friend,' he said.

Callis hurled himself into a roll, hearing the brass weapon-limb of the pursuing golem carve a ragged scar through the polished metal floor. He came up into a sprint, but staggered to a halt as he realised how close he was to the edge of the platform. A seemingly endless distance below him, the battle still raged. He caught a glimpse of islands of green-jacketed Iron Bulls, surrounded on all sides by a sea of enemies, but still fighting and dying hard. There was no time to survey the scene. He ducked instinctively and hurled himself to the side, resulting in the brass golem's blade arm whipping overhead. Callis scrambled away on all fours, desperately grabbing at Kazrug's pistol, knowing that it would be all but useless against this creature.

There was only one other thing to try. He ran once more towards the edge of the platform. The brass creature swivelled its head and came after him again. He backed up until he felt the rail against his back, raised his pistol and fired. The bullet skipped off the creature's metal hide.

'Come on then!' he roared. 'I'm right here!'

It charged, picking up speed as it came, raising the blades on its forelimbs to skewer him. He let it come closer. Closer.

At the last moment Callis hurled himself forwards. He slid on the polished floor, screaming like a madman as he went, sure that any moment now one of those blades would sink into his flesh.

They did not. The golem's wild swing overbalanced it, and as it tried to adjust, it staggered and crashed against the guardrail, which bent under the construct's weight. The golem teetered, trying to regain its balance, but it was simply too heavy. It hung in the air for an instant before toppling over the edge of the platform.

* * *

They both heard the groan of metal overhead. Vermyre looked up, and his eyes widened in horror before he hurled himself to the side. Toll was already rolling backwards, sure that he could not possibly get out of the way in time.

The brass automaton struck the floor with astonishing force, splintering the marble flagstones and sending a cloud of dust into the air. The shockwave knocked scores of guardsmen and cultists to the ground, and the sound was as deafening as the great church bells of the Abbey of Remembered Souls.

Toll could not hear a thing, but that did not matter. The world around him surged in slow motion, soldiers dragging themselves to their feet or silently screaming and clutching horrible wounds. Howling, bestial faces screeched through the clouds of dust. He ignored this all, trying to focus beyond the ringing in his ears and the pain in his skull.

He saw his target, stumbling blindly through the carnage. Toll bent and grasped the hilt of a broadsword that was buried in the chest of a dead cultist. He tore it free and began to run. Figures who stumbled into his path were shouldered out of the way. The ringing in Toll's ears was fading now, and he could hear the screams and chaos of battle all around. The fallen remains of the strange brass golem lay before him, and he climbed upon the thing's motionless back, sprinted up its spine and leapt from the twisted remnants of its head.

Ortam Vermyre turned and looked up, blood streaming from his ear and smeared across his face. The traitor's eyes went wide with shock.

'This is for Kazrug,' Toll snarled, savouring the traitor's fear.

His blade sliced through Vermyre's forearm with a sickening tearing sound, and the traitor's right hand, and the flaming sceptre it carried, clattered to the floor. Vermyre screamed and fell to his knees, clutching his bloody stump. The Witch Hunter moved to finish him off, raising his sword high. Before the blade could fall the stricken heretic tore something free of his neck, a gleaming sapphire stone bound on a golden cord. He crushed it in his hand and a concussive blast hurled Toll off his feet.

The shockwave created a visible circle of white-blue energy, and as Toll watched it rolled back in on itself before exploding in a vortex of shimmering azure as tall and wide as a man. The portal hung in the air, bleeding nauseating colours that flickered across the walls of the guildhall. Toll could hear a chorus of sibilant voices on the other side, whispering secrets and promises of eternal damnation. Vermyre stood, back to the portal, and let himself fall. As tendrils of spectral force wrapped themselves around his mutilated form, the former High Arbiter fixed his old friend with a hateful stare.

'I'll see you soon, Hanniver,' he promised.

The shimmering vortex collapsed in on itself in a kaleidoscope of impossible colours and half-formed shapes, and disappeared. No sign of Ortam Vermyre remained.

Around the Witch Hunter, the battle had devolved into a brutal, fractured melee. The remaining Knights Excelsior were islands of gleaming white in a riotous sea of colour. They fought like the heroes the legends depicted them to be. Cackling daemons hurled themselves at the giants' legs, trying to bear them down where they could be set upon by the swarm of avian beastmen. They would not fall. Every sweep of their swords sent enemies reeling and tumbling away, clutching at gaping wounds. They killed with their shields, smashing the foe to the floor and crushing skulls with powerful blows. And all the while they bellowed songs of praise to Sigmar, battle-hymns of devotion to their God-King.

For all their heroism, the enemy tide would not cease or relent. The fighting Iron Bulls of the Eighth were being picked apart, unable to maintain cohesion amidst the terrible fires and eldritch arrows of the beastmen.

Sentanus and his remaining warrior had the last golem down, and were taking it apart. The axe-wielding Stormcast raised his weapon high to strike the thing's head from its shoulders, but a blast of silver-white light struck him in the back. He was hurled away, smoke rising from a gaping hole seared through his armour. Kryn's laughter echoed above the clangour of the fighting below.

The White Reaper's pitiless mask snapped towards the mage, who was hovering in the air above the platform upon a disc of polished brass, his long, thin fingers already working the motions for another display of magic. Sentanus ignored the twitching pile of wreckage beneath him and raised his staff.

Too late. Kryn's hands thrust out at the Lord-Veritant, and once again the platform beneath them flowed and reformed. The half-destroyed golem melted into it, and the swirling metal wrapped around Sentanus' armoured legs, dragging him slowly, inexorably down.

'Even the mighty White Reaper, scourge of Excelsis, cannot stand before me,' said Kryn, floating closer on his metal disc, clapping in delight. 'Oh, your head will make a fine gift for my masters, Sentanus.'

He curled his fingers, and the flowing brass looped around the Reaper's throat and trapped his sword arm.

'It does not end with me, wizard,' spat Sentanus. He spoke the final word like a curse. 'Sigmar's faithful will never stop hunting you. You will burn, Kryn, I promise you, and the agony of your death will come as sweet relief after what came before it.'

Kryn's face twisted into a hateful scowl. The White Reaper's armour squealed as the brass bindings dug into it.

'Enough,' the wizened mage snarled. He raised his hands again, curled into talons.

Callis' pistol barked, and the shot struck Kryn in the chest. The wizard shrieked in surprise, his fury-filled eyes snapping towards the former corporal. Callis' heart sunk. Whatever magical wards the mage had summoned to protect himself had held.

'You dare?' Kryn hissed. 'I will tear the skin from your–'

The White Reaper's gauntleted fist snapped out, tearing apart the brass loops which bound his limbs and closing around Kryn's throat. The wizard's eyes almost popped out of his skull as he gasped and spluttered for breath, arms scrabbling weakly at the vice-like grip that held him.

'You are judged a heretic and a traitor to the one true god that is Sigmar,' Sentanus growled. He leaned forward, his pitiless mask an inch from the wizard's terrified, gasping face. 'Burn.'

The Lord-Veritant brought up his staff. The lantern flared. The blazing light enveloped Kryn's skull. His scream was one of purest agony. The mage's skin seared away in the face of that holy flame, his teeth blackening. The light grew brighter and brighter, until Callis had to look away.

The radiance faded. When he looked back, the White Reaper had hauled himself to his feet. The Lord-Veritant stared down at the smoking ashes that had once been Kryn. Wisps of smoke curled around the head of his lantern-staff.

The armoured giant's head turned towards Callis. He said nothing for a long time. Below, they could still hear the clash and cries of battle.

'Leave,' Sentanus said.

Without another word, the Lord-Veritant turned to stare up at the occulum fulgurest, which still rippled and arced with lightning that poured into the skies above the city. Sentanus raised his blade, and sliced one the great chains that held the occulum aloft.

With a deafening clatter of metal, the platform began to tilt and sway. Callis did not wait for a second word. Exhausted, he staggered towards the grand staircase.

With agonising slowness, the intricate working of the aetheric generator began to come apart, and the great sphere at the centre of the structure slipped from its chains and fell to the floor. The beastmen and daemons unfortunate enough to be directly below screeched and howled as they tried to claw their way out of its path, but it was too late. It crunched into the mass of bodies with an awful squelching sound, and a torrent of gore spurted out from beneath its colossal weight. The marble slabs of the floor shattered under that pressure, sending jagged shards whipping through the crowd. More of the machinery began to fall, mercifully missing the surviving soldiers.

'Forward, Iron Bulls,' came the voice of General Synor, who clearly recognised that the inexorable advance of the enemy had been halted by the death of their leader and the carnage of the falling occulum. 'Now is the time. Earn your glory, soldiers of Sigmar!'

Toll limped over. His face was bruised and bloodied, but otherwise he was unharmed. His rapier was drawn, and caked in congealing blood.

'Are you alright?' Synor asked. The general was holding a piece of torn cloth to a cut that ran from his jaw to just below his windpipe, narrowly avoiding carving his throat open. His voice was hoarse with pain, and blood ran freely down one of his shins. 'Fancy entering the fray again?'

In truth, he felt like lying there on the cool ground forever more, but the Witch Hunter nodded. His sword arm was useless, burned so badly that he could barely lift it without it sending a million red-hot needles dancing across his flesh, but by Sigmar he could still hold a gun.

'Ready to see this through,' he growled.

'Good show,' said the general, drawing his blade. 'Let's finish this.'

With the destruction of the corrupted machinery, the groundswell of foul sorcery that had begun to summon the crystal fortress into the skies above Excelsis was dispelled. There was a thunderous eruption that shattered every window in the city, and the colossal vortex that connected this realm with whatever tortured void had birthed the crystalline abomination vanished. The single spiral tower that had manifested entirely was sheared free from the structure that had secured it. It toppled from the sky in three separate pieces, striking the western quarter of the city. The spearhead that was the tip of the tower carved through the noble district, demolishing several of the palaces of the city's most powerful families. One of these buildings was the Palace of the High Arbiter, which was utterly obliterated in the cataclysmic power of the fall.

Another section crushed a large portion of the Veins, and the last crumpled a stretch of the city's great wall before exploding into fragments in the field in front of the city. Thousands died in the aftermath of the fall, yet countless more lives were saved with the destruction of the daemonic army that had besieged the city.

With the death of Kryn and the disappearance of the High Arbiter, as well as the banishment of the great portal in the sky, whatever chains of sorcery binding the daemonic legions of Tzeentch to the Realm of Beasts were sundered, gibbering abominations faded and disappeared, exploded into clouds of violent colours, or simply melted in on themselves. Shorn of their daemonic support, the Cult of the Fated Path and their feral allies were encircled and destroyed. The loyal survivors of the City Guard regiments showed no mercy, and the slaughter carried on long into the night. General Synor personally slew the chieftain of the beastmen in single combat, earning yet another scroll of honour for the mighty Eighth.

As with any battle, there was no clean ending. The Firewolves, who had been encircled and ambushed by the traitorous Coldguard, were decimated by volleys of rifle and cannon fire. Hundreds of warriors were slain in moments, and General Revard was dragged from his horse and butchered. By the time the insurrection fell apart, and a troop of duardin irregulars had arrived to relieve them, the Firewolves had been reduced to a mere seventy-five men and women. The regiment was dead. Try as they might, the remaining armies of the city could not hunt down every single cultist heretic, and many took advantage of the chaos of battle to slink back into the shadows, once more taking up their civilian identities. The warriors of the Knights Excelsior wasted no time in surrounding and guarding the fallen pieces of the crystal tower. The remnants of the Coldguard regiment, judged to be corrupted beyond hope of redemption, were rounded up and led to the dreaded Consecralium. The screams of the dying echoed across the city for many nights, and the legend of the White Reaper's ruthlessness only grew.

General Synor's office was a far different place than it had been before the battle of Excelsis. The fine whalebone desk, once covered with decanters and cigars, was now home to several imposing towers of parchment – maps, official-looking letters with a colourful variety of intricate wax seals, and all manner of other bureaucratic ephemera.

Callis opened the door, ducking past a flush-faced guardsman carrying a crate full of deep-green uniform long coats. Inside, the room was hazy with spice-smoke, and the curtains had been pulled closed to cut out the midday sun. Synor sat behind the desk, a bandage wrapped around his wounded neck.

'Ah, corporal,' he said, rising from his chair with a visible wince. His leg was splinted and heavily bound. 'I'm glad you came. Please, take a seat.'

Callis obliged. He gazed over the documents spread out before him. Dispatch notices for various infantry formations. Maps of the local area. Records of destroyed or lost equipment that needed to be replaced.

'Believe me, this is nothing,' said Synor, uncorking a fresh bottle. 'The city's a mess. We've got half our soldiers missing or dead, a fair portion of the city burnt to ashes, and the Reaper looming over our companies looking for a reason to string up the rest of us.'

'I don't envy you, sir,' said Callis. 'I suppose it's little comfort that things could have been a fair deal worse.'

Synor snorted. 'Perhaps. Personally I would find it hard to choose between a violent death and having to fill out another requisition order.'

'Don't you have an orderly to take care of that, sir?'

'I had several. All of them were killed during the fighting. Believe me, you don't appreciate the help until they're gone.'

The general poured fine amber spirit into two glasses, and offered one to Callis. The former corporal shook his head.

'I'll cut to the quick,' said Synor, slumping back down into his chair. 'After the madness of the last few days, I find myself very short of good men. Men with initiative. I know that we hardly got off to the best start, corporal, but having the sky fall in on your head and your city burn around you will clear the mind of any man. The truth is that I misjudged you, and I'm man enough to apologise for that.'

'You're offering to reinstate me?'

'No. I'm offering you a commission. Lieutenant. You'll be responsible for your own platoon.'

Callis blinked in surprise. A commission? Sigmar's teeth, that was far beyond what he had expected. Few but the richest Azyrite youths could afford to pay for an officer's stripes. Those like Callis, descended from the reclaimed tribes of the Coast of Tusks, had to do it the hard way, rising up and up through the ranks over the course of a long career. This was the sort of opportunity he had never even dreamed of.

'That's... I don't know what to say, general,' he said, shaking his head.

'Say yes. You're a bright lad, and you can fight. I need fighters. Right now Excelsis is vulnerable, corporal, and every blood-sucking predator and petty warlord on this filth-pit of a continent is going to smell that weakness. I need new men, and I need new officers to lead those men.'

He drained his glass, and fished his spice-pipe from his jacket. The smell of the damned thing was awful, like burnt hair mixed with cheap perfume. Callis did his best not to breathe in. Spewing up all over the general's desk would probably not be the best way to secure his promotion. Synor rummaged through the documents on the desk, liberally smothering everything in foul-smelling ash. He hurled a cluster of curled, yellow scrolls aside, and grabbed a small wooden box. He flipped it towards Callis.

'There are your stripes. I'll expect you to report here at the crack of dawn tomorrow. We'll go over all the necessaries then. Until then, take the afternoon off. Spend a few glimmerings. There'll be precious little time for leisure in the coming months.'

Callis turned the box over in his hands, and stood up to take his leave. Synor was already scrabbling through the detritus before him, piling documents haphazardly on separate piles, dragging back on his pipe furiously. All in all, not the most glamorous advertisement for a career in the military. Callis felt oddly hollow as he closed the door behind him. This was what he had wanted for years now, toiling away under the command of incompetents and blowhards, thinking of all the things he'd do differently in their place.

Now that long sought-after promotion was, quite literally, in the palm of his hand. And he felt nothing but a vague sense of melancholy and a wave of crushing tiredness.

It was blazing hot again. Lieutenant Armand Callis shrugged at the sweat-soaked jacket he wore, trying to adjust the thick material until he was halfway comfortable. This was the trouble with being a ranking officer – you had to try and look like one.

The heat was not the only issue. He looked out across the collection of rogues and miscreants he had been handed. Two weeks of drilling dawn to dusk, wearing them down with endless training exercises and physical fitness examinations, and they still resembled a gang of gangly youths who had accidentally stumbled across a wardrobe full of soldiers' uniforms. He walked down the line, baton in hand. Guardsman Korgis had a shiny pair of black eyes and an impressively swollen lip.

'Guardsman,' he growled through gritted teeth. 'I believe I told you that the next time you got drunk and started a brawl I would hang you from the top of the harbour wall by your most treasured organs.'

Korgis' eyes flicked nervously back and forth.

'Not been fighting, sir,' he said, his words rendered barely intelligible by his battered jaw.

'Would you like to explain, then, why it looks like you have spent the last few days headbutting a stone wall?'

The guardsman's eyes furrowed in concentration. There was a silence that stretched on uncomfortably long.

'Tripped?' he offered at last.

Callis sighed.

'You're on latrine duty for the next week,' he said. 'You can start right now.'

Guardsman Korgis' battered face fell, and he strode off towards the barracks, shoulders slumped. Callis shook his head. They needed a war to fight.

'The rest of you,' he bellowed, trying to get that same air of disgusted rage that old Happer had managed to capture so well. 'Three circuits of the arms yard. Get moving.'

His collection of awkward youths and cauliflower-eared trouble-makers began to half-heartedly jog. Callis could not even be bothered to threaten them into taking the exercise more seriously. He moved over to the shade of the bastion's perimeter wall, and watched the fighting third platoon stagger around the yard.

'Now that's an imposing collection of warriors,' came a voice at his side.

It was Toll. He was leaning against the wall a few steps away, turning his wide-brimmed hat around in his hands. Callis was surprised at how good it felt to see the man. He guessed a certain amount of camaraderie was to be expected after the hardships they had endured together.

'Ruthless killers to a man,' said Callis, approaching the Witch Hunter. 'We lost a lot of good men in the battle. Have to find new recruits from somewhere.'

Toll nodded. 'Congratulations on the promotion, by the way. Sorry I missed you after the fighting. I was… otherwise engaged. Fulfilling the last request of an old friend.'

'I'm sorry for what happened to Kazrug,' said Callis, softly. 'I didn't know him long, but he seemed a good sort.'

Toll gave a brief nod, but said nothing more. They stood in silence for a while, watching Callis' men do their circuits. A few of them were kicking each other's ankles, trying to trip each other up. Callis sighed.

'You know, I'm glad,' said Toll.

'Of what?'

'That you've got the look of a man who's bored out of his skull and deeply regretting the career choices he's made.'

Callis shook his head. 'I'm not, that's not what–'

'You're not a soldier any more,' said the Witch Hunter, ignoring Callis' half-hearted indignation. 'You've seen behind the veil. You've faced down one of the countless evils that want to pull this world we're creating down around us. Training rookie guardsmen is not going to compare.'

'I'm just a soldier, Hanniver. This is where I belong.'

'We're all just common men and women, Armand. That's what the Order is. We're not the monsters the people believe us to be. We have no magical powers. All we have is our wit, our fortitude and our determination to destroy those who would corrupt and destroy the new world that the God-King is building across the realms.'

'What are you asking of me?' said Callis, honestly confused. 'It's good to see you, but I'm not sure why you're here.'

'My superiors have a new task for me,' said Toll, stepping away from the wall and placing his familiar wide-brimmed hat upon his head. 'I find myself without a companion at my side, and it's a sad truth that there are not many souls in this city I trust. Not any more. You, however, I am pretty sure are not going to knife me in the back.'

'Thanks very much.'

'I am offering you a position at my side. You're quick-witted, and decent in a fight. You know the city, and you know the dangers we face.'

'I'm a lieutenant now. In charge of my own platoon,' Callis said. 'I can't just drop everything and leave.'

'If you value any kind of stability in your life, I suggest you don't,' said Toll. 'Let's make something clear here – if you join me, the pay will be bad, the leisure time will be extremely limited, and it'll be a quiet week indeed if no one tries to kill you. This is also a time-sensitive matter, so you'd have to abandon your post right now if you were to come with me. That's desertion, as I'm sure you're aware.'

'You're not exactly selling this to me, Hanniver.'

Toll shrugged. 'All I can say is that at my side, you'll be doing Sigmar's work. Heretics and traitors like Vermyre? Madmen like Kryn who would see this world burn in exchange for just a glimpse of power? We are the sword poised above their necks. And there is nothing quite so satisfying as watching such men fall.'

Callis shook his head, but said nothing. What did he really want? The last couple of weeks had been hellishly dull, an endless parade of training and drills, punctuated by visits to the officer's mess, where they shunned him as a jumped-up native who had been promoted above his ability and birth. On the other hand, he had always been a soldier. That was all he knew. How could he just abandon that and stride off into Sigmar alone knew what kind of life?

Toll let the silence stretch out. There was a faint grin on his lips, as if he already knew what the lieutenant would say, and was only waiting for the words to be spoken.

Callis stared out across the drill yard. Six or seven of his men were standing hands on hips, red-faced and wheezing. On the far side of the yard, Lieutenant Donalholme was bellowing directly into the face of a young recruit, while Lieutenant Franc looked on, not even bothering to hide his gleeful smirk. On the walls above, bored soldiers leaned on their halberds, staring out over the city.

He turned to Toll.

'Fine, but you'll have to write me one hell of a resignation letter,' he said.

ABOUT THE AUTHOR

Nick Horth is the author of the Age of Sigmar novella *City of Secrets* and the novel *Callis & Toll: The Silver Shard*. Nick works as a background writer for Games Workshop, crafting the worlds of Warhammer Age of Sigmar and Warhammer 40,000. He lives in Nottingham, UK.

EIGHT LAMENTATIONS: SPEAR OF SHADOWS
Josh Reynolds

Eight mighty artefacts, crafted by the dark servants of Chaos, blight the Mortal Realms. The Ruinous Powers hunt them – and so do a group of heroes, chosen by Grungni for this dangerous and essential task.